Secret of Epping Forest
Bridget Kathleen

Illustration by Raluca Andreea Porumbacu

To my big brother, Joshua David,
You were our Sunshine, our only Sunshine.

Prologue

On a summer night—any night, really—a solitary mansion sits deep in a forest in England. Its front yard is littered with tiny, colorful flowers; sparse patches of grass dot the unkempt grounds. The brawny oak front doors sit silently. They long to be opened, their intricately etched design gone unnoticed for far too long.

The moon does its best to shine down on the mansion's withering magnificence, but the trees shield it from view, hiding it from the world. The mansion sits there, untouched, like a forbidden treasure. The trails that once led to it are long gone, having been reclaimed by Mother Nature. No one comes to visit anymore; no one cares to, not for over a hundred years.

The mansion sits there desolate with no one to disturb it, though it wants to be disturbed. It welcomes any guest adventurous enough—or brave enough—to take a gander. It has grown older, sinking deeper and deeper in on itself. Finally, the realization of total isolation takes its toll. Perhaps no one will ever walk its beautiful halls or gardens again. What was once a grand home now slowly turns to waste on what will soon become its grave. But, as the night becomes morning, the mansion creaks, waking up.

The air is still cool. The dew covering the grass and flowers acts as a mirror, and the mansion sees its old reflection once again. The bricks are chipped, and half the windows are broken or boarded up. The view of it says to stay away, but from the inside the mansion pleads: come take a look at me! The mansion shelters a powerful secret, one that protects its identity. Because of that secret, the mansion fears it will never be loved again.

As morning turns into midday, the grass and the dirt and the flowers soak up the dew. Even as the sun beats down on the trees, the mansion is still well hidden from prying eyes. A mother deer walks with her babies.

They sniff the front gates. And then, quite suddenly, the mother deer and her babies run off, as if scared by something. For a moment it is quiet, and the mansion heaves a heavy sigh. But all too soon, it looks like, as a teenage girl with long, pretty auburn hair stumbles upon its gates. The mansion gazes down at the girl as she gazes up at it in bewilderment. For so long, the mansion has waited for this moment, begged for this moment, for a visitor to look at it in awe.

The girl grasps the gates with both hands and pushes them open. She grimaces as the rusty metal creaks, but to the mansion it couldn't have sounded more beautiful. And with every step the girl took, the mansion watched—always it watched. The girl looked this way and that, as if she had never seen something so astonishing in all her life. And perhaps she hadn't.

As the girl made her way up to the front doors, she looked up as high as she could and smiled at the mansion, her dark-blue eyes twinkling. At long last she rested her hands on the front doors and pushed with all her might.

"Hello?"

Her voice echoed throughout the mansion, breathing new life into it.

Chapter One

It was the middle of May when Rose Fair first arrived in London. She clutched her giant, dark-blue suitcase, which almost matched the color of her eyes, and followed closely behind her parents. Just a few months ago she never had a passport, never traveled anywhere because her parents were always too busy, and never went anywhere besides on school field trips. Now that Rose had graduated, a trip to just about anywhere was out of her reach, well, until last month when her parents presented her with her very first passport. She had a month to get ready, her parents said, for this was her graduation gift from the two of them.

Rose patted her shoulder bag, the imprint of her passport still there. She relaxed some only to be stirred seconds later as her father's voice shouted out to the city life of London for a taxi. Her mother looked back at her and motioned with her head for Rose to hurry up. She set her large suitcase to the side and let her father load it into the trunk of the taxi, along with the rest of their luggage.

"Where to?" the taxi driver asked.

"The Crest of Feathers in Loughton, please," said Rose's father.

The taxi driver smiled and nodded. "Up by the Epping Forest, I see. Have you been there before?"

Rose's father gave a quick nod. "It was a long time ago, yes; before this one was born." He gestured toward Rose, making her feel more uncomfortable as she sat squished between her parents.

"What a beautiful daughter," the taxi man commented. "You're very blessed."

"Thank you," Rose's mother replied softly.

Rose was not only uncomfortable but extremely tired. She had been up for more than twenty-four hours and had slept little the night before leaving, for she was both nervous and excited about crossing the Atlantic to England. Now she was stuck in a taxi for the next thirty minutes with very little leg room.

Luckily, the drive was over before she fell asleep. When they arrived, she stretched her cramped limbs and welcomed the fresh air. She was handed her suitcase by her father as her mother paid the taxi driver.

The Crest of Feathers was a local diner. Rose had imagined it would look old, like the town, but she guessed she shouldn't have been surprised, for there was more to England than tall towers and castles. Nevertheless, this was not what she had been hoping for.

A happy squeal brought her back to reality, and Rose turned to see a man and a woman walking toward them. Her parents welcomed them with open arms and gave them a long hug.

"It's so good to see you again, Luke," said the brown-bearded, middle-aged fellow. He was tall with broad shoulders and stood a head taller than Rose's father. "I hope your flight was good. Any jet lag?" he asked.

Luke shook his head. "No, surprisingly," He looked over his shoulder and glanced at Rose. "However, I think my daughter feels a little bit different."

Rose, pulling her suitcase behind her, stood next to her father and held out her hand to the man. "Hi, I'm Rose."

The bearded man laughed and smiled broadly as he took her hand. "It's nice to meet you, Rose. My name is Alan." He practically crushed her hand, but, of course, he didn't mean to. When it came to Rose's petite frame, anything looked like it might crush her. "And this is my wife, Diana."

The short, stout woman walked up to Rose and gently shook her hand. "It's nice to finally meet you, Rose. I've only seen photos and heard

4

stories about you. You're even prettier in person."

Rose blushed at this and smiled awkwardly.

"Let's head inside," said Rose's mother. "I'm starved."

Diana nodded in agreement. "Tiffany has the right idea; let's eat."

For starters they had bread, oil, and olives. It was warm ciabatta bread with extra virgin olive oil and Aspall's apple balsamic with mixed marinated olives and Maldon sea salt. Even though she was hungry, Rose, not wanting to seem rude, took only a few bites and instead saved her hunger for the main meal.

It might have been twelve in the afternoon in England, but to Rose it felt much later. All she wanted to do was lie down and sleep. Thankfully, her tea helped keep her from dozing off.

"I'm so glad you decided to stay in Loughton," said Diana, adding with delight, "Maybe you'll catch a glimpse of a ghost in the Epping Forest."

Luke laughed. "There is no such thing as ghosts, Diana." Of course, he meant that in the nicest way possible.

Diana scoffed and continued talking about it. "That's too bad, Luke. Life is no fun without a little supernatural." She cleared her throat. "Anyway, the Epping Forest is one of the most haunted forests in England. Best stay at the edge of it; otherwise you might be spirited away!"

Rose almost spat out her tea.

"Did I say something funny?" Diana asked.

Tiffany shook her head. "No, you didn't. It's just that, Rose doesn't really believe in the supernatural either."

Diana seemed disappointed. "What a shame." She sighed.

At long last their food arrived. To Rose it seemed to have taken an eternity, but when she saw her food, she knew that it had been worth the wait. The Yorkshire ham, egg, and chips made her mouth water, the first bite sending a boost of energy through her body. With a place to stretch her legs, good food, and a refreshing drink, Rose felt re-energized now.

Alan wiped his mouth with a napkin and looked over at Rose. "How old are you, Rose?"

Rose was caught in mid-chew and hurriedly finished eating before answering. "I'll be nineteen next month."

Alan smiled. "We'll have to do something for your special day then."

Rose nodded in agreement as the rest of the conversation was overtaken by the adults, and Rose found herself enjoying the last of her meal in silence. So far, she had seen the busy life of London and caught sight of Big Ben and even parts of the countryside, but still no castles or old ruins, which was what she had hoped for.

When lunch was over, Rose and her parents hauled their luggage into their friends' car and piled inside. Once again Rose felt as though she was back on the plane, although thankfully, the drive to their destination was less than ten minutes.

Alan took a sharp right and headed down a bumpy, narrow dirt road. Rose thought for sure they would get stuck or maybe even collide with another vehicle. The hills doubled in size, towering over the car as they drove, and tall grasses further infringed on their already narrow pathway. In time, they came to a wide dirt path. On one side lay the hills and the tall grass, and on the other side stood trees. Is this Epping Forest, Rose thought?

Their last turn was another right, and a single rugged path lay before them. Alan explained that no one had been down it for years, so the road was littered with twigs and broken branches and dead leaves. Alan drove slowly, maneuvering around the debris. He even had to move a large branch that had fallen from a rotting tree. Luke helped, of course.

When they finally reached the house, Rose was not disappointed. An eighteenth-century brick two-story stood a few yards from her as she got out of the car. Vegetation had overtaken half of the house. The only thing that looked somewhat new was the door.

"I'll help you with that," said Alan, taking Rose's large suitcase and unlocking the door.

Rose walked inside only to see that much of the interior had been remodeled. Antique wallpaper and woodwork still covered the walls, but everything else had been modernized.

"All of the furniture has changed," Diana said. "They do it every couple of years, so you won't see anything familiar from the last time you stayed here."

Rose looked to her parents. "You stayed in this house the last time you were here?"

Tiffany nodded and stood next to her daughter. "I hope you'll like it here. Without this place I'm not sure we would have been able to make the trip. Hotels can be so expensive."

"How much is it to stay here?" Rose asked.

"Not one penny," Lucas said. "It was all free. Diana and Alan rent this house out to people traveling, but since we're old friends, we can stay here for free."

Rose gasped. "Are you serious?" She couldn't believe she was going to be staying in such a beautiful home for free for the rest of the summer.

Tiffany smiled at her daughter's bemusement. "Go pick out a room, and Alan will help carry your suitcase."

Exhausted, Rose slogged her way upstairs. There were so many doors to so many rooms, she wasn't sure where to begin. One looked like the master bedroom, so she left it for her parents and continued on. Each room was so beautifully decorated that it was hard to choose. Rose glanced over her shoulder and saw Alan patiently waiting for her to decide. She bit her lower lip, trying to make up her mind as quickly as possible. Eventually, she chose a room near the end of a hall. The walls, adorned with paintings of landscapes and photographed portraits from centuries past, were decorated in light pink and trimmed in faded green vines and blue flowers. The only floor covering was a smoky brown rug under the bed. The bed sat between two windows; a sky-blue blanket and lace-trimmed white pillows seemed to call her name. Across from the bed was a white dresser with a mirror attached to it.

"Is this the one?" asked Alan.

Rose, smiling shyly, turned to face him. "Thank you," she said, then took her suitcase. Alan gave her a playful wink. "Better get some rest. It looks like you need it." He closed the door behind him, and Rose was finally alone, which was what she had been wanting ever since she got off the plane.

Standing in front of the mirror, she saw the dark circles under her eyes and the braid in her hair beginning to fall out. Alan was right; it did look as if she needed the rest. She didn't even bother unpacking. Instead, she went straight to bed and fell sound sleep.

Rose slept for the rest of the day and all through the night until early morning. She was still in the same position as when she had fallen asleep, only this time her pillow was wet with drool. Sitting up slowly, she rubbed her eyes, yawned, and stretched as the morning sun filtered through the curtains. Feeling refreshed, she opened her suitcase and grabbed her hairbrush, toothbrush, and toothpaste, and a clean set of clothes, then hurried down the hall to find a bathroom and take a long, much deserved bath. Grabbing the bar of soap, she brought it up to her nose. It smelled like lavender, and she lathered her body in it. Her hair still smelled clean despite her travels, so she decided to wash it later.

After washing up and brushing her teeth, Rose went downstairs, hoping to find her parents, but the house was quiet. "Mom, Dad, are you here?" The only sound she heard was the soft ticking of the grandfather clock.

When Rose walked into the kitchen, she found a note on a yellow pad on the counter. It read: Good morning, Rose. Breakfast is in the fridge. Your dad and I went out with Diana and Alan again. We will be back before dinner. Take this time to relax. Love, Mom.

Rose opened the fridge and pulled out the leftover pancakes. She poured maple syrup and powdered sugar on top, and to finish it off she cut up strawberries and laid them prettily around the edge of the plate of pancakes.

Afterward, she roamed around the rest of the house, looking into the other bedrooms to confirm she had chosen the right one for her. Suddenly, the house creaked, and Rose's head jerked upward. The house was settling, but it still left her feeling unnerved. It's just a really old house, thought Rose; nothing to be scared about. And she didn't believe in ghosts, anyway, so the house being haunted was just a silly thought.

She returned to her room and grabbed her phone. Her plan was to get in touch with her friends back in America, but there was no access to internet, so Rose set her phone down with a sigh.

The house settled again, startling Rose. "Old houses do this all the time," she assured herself. Nevertheless, she stepped out into the hallway again to listen. The house did not creak this time, but something else did. Rose turned her head in the direction of the noise and followed after it. For a second she thought that maybe it was a spirit of a former resident. But, no surprise to her, she scoffed at that notion. The noise was now coming from a door left slightly ajar. As she walked down the hall to close it, the door swung all the way open.

Before her stood a flight of stairs, which she walked up gingerly. Every step creaked, and there were no railings to grab. When she reached the top, she forced open the door. The hinges had frozen in place after not being used for so long, and the dust was so bad that she began coughing and finally decided to pull up her shirt and cover her mouth and nose until the dust subsided.

The room was packed with old cardboard boxes and antique chests. Objects were covered in white sheets, but Rose dared not pull one off in case she would get shrouded in dust again. Instead, she closed the door and returned to the first floor to see if her parents had returned. They hadn't, and she grew restless. Finally, the thought of the forest came to mind, and she walked outside and to the back of the property. The ground was wet, and the smell of rain hit her nose. It must have rained in the night, but she was in too deep a sleep to have heard it.

As Rose walked to the edge of the forest, the still-wet grass kissed her skinny jeans, but she didn't mind. Rose was too wrapped up in what she was seeing before her. A new world was played out right in front of her eyes, and it was free for her to explore. I won't go far, she promised herself, just a quick peek, and she vanished into the forest.

If the supernatural world did exist, Rose didn't care about stepping on its territory. She was too enchanted by the beauty of the forest. The sights, the sounds, the whole atmosphere clung to Rose like spilled glitter. She knew she was taking a step toward a new chapter in her life. Where that road would lead her was a mystery.

The forest had much to offer, but Rose would have to discover it first. Though her shoes were caked in mud, the wind had picked up and the once-blue skies were turning gray, Rose didn't want to turn around yet.

The screech of a far-off animal spooked her as she walked in the opposite direction. Perhaps now was a good time to leave, and maybe her parents had returned.

As she walked, she came upon an overgrown trail and thought it might lead back to the main road. But the trail eventually disappeared, leaving Rose hopelessly lost. She pushed through thick bushes and irritably snapped pesky twigs that got in her way. Just when her efforts seemed to be in vain, she tripped over a root and fell onto another trail.

"Okay," she said. "This has to lead me back." This trail was wider than the last, so she had high hopes that it would bring her back to the main road. But, alas, as she came close to what appeared to be the edge of the forest, she was met with another surprise.

Standing before her was a grand mansion. A worn brick fence circled it, and its big, black gates stood firm so as to keep out any and all intruders. Rose stood in awe for a moment, then gripped the gates with both hands and pushed with all her might, surprised that they opened, though grudgingly. Their loud creaking made her cringe.

Inside the gates, Rose could get a better look at the mansion. Some of the windows were broken or boarded up, and she didn't know if anyone still lived there. She thought that maybe someone was trying to fix it up, since it seemed as if one side of the mansion was charred. Whatever or whoever was inside, Rose would find out. She pressed her palms flat against the two doors and looked up with a look of satisfaction. Without another thought she opened the doors and made her way inside. Rose couldn't help but think something was telling her to come inside and see what it had to offer. "Hello?" she called out, but there was no reply.

When she entered, Rose half expected to find the place covered in dust, dirt, and animal droppings. Instead, the place was clean, as if someone had just recently been here. She looked at her shoes and felt guilty for tracking in mud. But if no one was here, then surely it would be okay to walk around in dirty shoes. If anyone was there cleaning, she reasoned, she would just apologize and remove her shoes. But until that time came …

She walked up a wide flight of stairs, the steps covered with a large, worn red rug. The stairs eventually split off in two directions, and Rose climbed each side to see where it led. The walls were decorated with old paintings and stubs of candles sitting on broken wooden stands. Some vases held fresh flowers, while others had flowers so dry that they looked as if they would crumble with a single touch.

The dark oak railings were etched with eye-catching designs, and doors on the farthest walls led to other areas of the mansion. There was simply too much to explore for Rose to see in just one day; she would have to come back soon. Before continuing, she looked up at the faded ceiling and gasped in amazement. Rose could make out a magnificent painting of the sky with naked angels holding hands in a circle. For a second, she could only wonder who could have painted such a beautiful scene.

As Rose opened each door, she wasn't at all surprised to find the rooms completely covered in dust and cobwebs. Several rooms were empty —not a single chair or piece of clothing left behind. Perhaps whoever lived here was moving out, or maybe moving in. As the minutes passed, Rose found what she had hoped for: a music room. Her mother was a music teacher, and Rose had the opportunity to practice the piano whenever she wanted. She had started at a young age, so she was able to read music notes and play a great number of songs. Of all the things Rose had seen so far in the mansion, the music room was the tidiest. Not a speck of dirt could be found on the piano or anything else lying in the room.

The piano keys beckoned Rose to touch them. She sat down on the wooden seat, its velvet cushion so worn in places that the material was ripping. This didn't bother Rose, who was used to sitting on a hard bench. She gently caressed each key with her fingers and started playing a favorite tune from memory. Mellow music filled the room, and she closed her eyes as she played. Suddenly, she stopped, the sense of time coming back to her, and she cursed under her breath.

Exploring the rest of the mansion would have to wait for another day. I wonder if Mom and Dad are back yet, Rose thought. She had no idea what time it was and hadn't bother to take her phone because it was no good to her here in England except to take photos. And with no internet access, checking her social status was out of the question. Finding her way home would not be easy, though, as she had a hard-enough time trying to find this place. It had been just luck that she stumbled upon it.

Rose glanced at the sky through the thick leaves and branches and noticed the gray skies had cleared and the sun was almost overhead. She noticed in the morning which way the back of the house faced and decided to head that way, thinking she was bound to reach the edge of the forest sooner or later.

Rose's attempt to walk back was a struggle. After falling for a second time, there was no doubt she would have to bathe again, and this time wash her hair. Her choice of clothes didn't help either; her bare arms felt itchy, and she kept getting bit by bugs. At least she wore jeans, but they were wet with mud splatters on them, and her poor shoes had slim chance of surviving the rest of the day.

Suddenly, she spotted someone standing a few feet from her. The stranger was a few inches shorter than her and wore what appeared to be a black cloak. Her foot snapped a twig, and the person turned to look at her.

"Hi." Rose was surprised to see that it was young boy. "Could you help me?" she asked.

The little boy nodded. He couldn't have been older than twelve.

"I'm staying in a house not far from here. Do you know where it is?" She felt silly asking a youngster for directions.

The boy nodded. He looked uncomfortable, as if he had been caught doing something wrong. He pointed to his left and said: "If you keep going straight, you'll come across a house. I'm sure that's the one you're talking about."

A wave of relief washed over Rose, and she smiled. "Oh, thank you so much."

This time the boy smiled, but just a little. "You're welcome, miss."

Rose shyly waved goodbye and started to make her way back to the house. As she kept the light of the sun on her right shoulder, she couldn't help but think that the boy seemed rather odd. He was only her second encounter with someone in the United Kingdom; Diana and Alan were the first, so Rose wasn't sure how the average British citizen acted; TV shows and movies didn't count.

Finally, the house came into view through the gaps in the trees, and Rose popped out into the back yard. She took in a deep breath and gave an exasperated sigh. Relieved that her parents were not yet home, she headed upstairs to shower, but not before leaving her shoes outside on the back doorstep.

The water from the shower was cool and refreshing. The itching had finally stopped. She scrubbed the dirt from her skin, picked the mud from beneath her fingernails, and washed her hair twice to get back that nice, silky feel.

Just as Rose was finishing up, she heard a faint humming sound. She turned off the faucet and wrung the water from her hair before stepping out of the shower. The faint humming continued, and Rose thought that maybe her parents were home. She wrapped herself in a towel before opening the bathroom door a crack to listen in the hall for the humming. It was still faint, but Rose could hear it better. "Hello?" she called out.

The humming stopped.

"Mom, Dad, is that you? Diana? Alan?" But there was no reply.

Without warning, something cool touched her cheek. Rose flinched and slammed the door shut. "There's no such thing as ghosts." Rose kept telling herself this only to jump again when she thought she heard someone sigh behind her. Rose laughed, feeling uneasy. It's just jet lag, she told herself. She was staying in a strange house in a strange land and thought for sure that was what was making her hear things.

Before completely losing her mind, Rose heard her mother's laughter. Finally calmed down, she quickly dressed to greet her parents.

Tiffany and Luke were downstairs in the living room talking with Alan and Diana. They had spent the day catching up on the old days. By this time it was nearly five o'clock, and hunger was settling in again. Rose would have packed a lunch before going into the forest, but there was little food in the fridge.

Tiffany saw Rose standing near the doorway and rushed over to. "We were thinking of eating out for supper. Until we go to the grocery store there's not much we can do. How about it? Do you mind eating with a few oldies?"

Her stomach growling, Rose nodded. She had no problem eating with a couple of adults, especially if the food was free. "Where are we eating?"

They ate at a place called The Green Tree. It was a modern Mediterranean restaurant with a chill ambience. Rose felt as if she was back home in California. And since she was well rested and clean, she could actually enjoy herself, relaxing in the chair and not caring if she slouched.

"We'll have to go grocery shopping first thing tomorrow." Luke said as he opened his menu.

Tiffany snapped her fingers. "You're right." Turning to Rose, "Do you want to come? You can pick out some food to eat during the week."

Rose thought about it for a moment, then said, "Maybe, if I'm awake, yeah. If not, just grab some stuff you think I might like." Rose doubted she would be up by the time her parents left the house. She wasn't an early bird and preferred to sleep in when she got the chance. She appreciated that her parents offered and always took kindly to the opportunities they presented to her.

Diana smiled mischievously. "So, have you run into any ghosts yet?"

Rose would have chuckled at this if not for the fact that she had encountered some strange things that day. "No, I haven't. I'll let you know when I do, though." She felt the need to leave out the bit about the mansion and hearing humming when no one else was around. She didn't want to feed into the idea.

Diana was a bit disappointed. "Oh well. There are plenty of other things to see here in England." She clapped her hands suddenly and said, "We'll have to go to Canvey Island and visit the beach before you go."

Luke rubbed his chin, looking thoughtful. "Canvey Island, huh. I can't remember the last time I was there."

Tiffany looked to Rose. "We could have your birthday party there. Or maybe you want to go shopping in London?"

Rose nodded at this. Both were great ideas, but then she suggested, "Or maybe a castle?"

Alan laughed, getting her hint. "If it's castles you want to see, I can suggest a few favorites."

Rose nodded, intrigued.

Alan started counting with his fingers as he named off castles. "The Bodiam, Warwick, Leeds, Dover. All are within a reasonable distance from here. In fact, we could visit the beach near Dover castle. It would be a win-win."

16

The prospect of seeing castles and visiting beaches excited Rose; she just hoped she had time for all of it.

The next morning she did not get up in time to go shopping with her parents. Instead, she pulled the covers over her head and slept in. It wasn't long, though, before she sat up, feeling hungry again, but she wasn't sure if there was any food for breakfast. Perhaps she should have gone with her parents.

Rose looked at herself in the mirror. Her face was puffy as she cleared the sleep from her eyes. After brushing her teeth and pulling her hair back into a ponytail, she put on clothes more suitable for running around in the forest. As she stepped out into the hallway, again the door to the attic was creaking. She was sure she had closed it good and tight. Perhaps one of her parents had been up there.

When Rose went to close the attic door, she noticed a white sheet lying on the steps. Curious, she picked up the sheet to put it back in its rightful place, but when she looked up, she saw that the main attic door was swinging back and forth. Rose tried to convince herself that it was just the wind and that it must happen all the time. Surely, there was nothing wrong.

As she stepped foot inside the attic again, she found the problem: a window had been broken, giving the wind easy access to blow things around. Perhaps a bird had flown into the glass.

Rose found what was missing its sheet. It was a painting half the size of her of a rosy-cheeked young woman with wavy, blond hair styled in an 19th-century updo. Its dark wooden frame was chipped at the corners. "Wow," Rose said as she took a closer look. "She's beautiful."

Rose caught herself admiring the painting and laid the sheet back over it. As she was ready to leave, she walked over to another sheet-covered object. It was a crate. Rose got down on her hands and knees and tried to pry the lid open. She had nearly given up when the crate snapped open, and a squeal escaped her lips as she lost hold of the handle.

Inside were old books, letters, and maps. Rose reached in and gingerly grabbed one of the letters. The paper was stiff, and Rose was afraid it would be too brittle to unfold. She put it back in the crate and grabbed another. This rolled-up piece of paper had a softer texture, and Rose could easily open it. The letter began:

To my dearest Elizabeth,

I can only pray that you are doing well. The winter has been hard on us all and the little ones miss you so...

The letters started to fade, and Rose grabbed another rolled-up letter. It read:

To my dearest Elizabeth,

I've started a school for young boys; and girls, too! I want everyone to have an education. My father always used to say: the key to a bright future is an education. I wish I could see the look on your face right now as you read this. I am sure you are smiling from ear to ear. I am smiling too.

The words started to fade, and all that Rose could make out at the bottom corner were a few letters of a person's name. Her stomach growled at that moment, so she put the letter back into the crate, and with the lid closed, covered it with the sheet.

On her way down to the kitchen, she found a bowl of fruit and devoured an apple to its core. She also wrapped some fruit inside a washcloth. If she was going into the forest again, she wanted food in case she got hungry. Before leaving, she grabbed her phone so she could take photos and left a quick note explaining where she was.

Rose took her time taking pictures in the forest. At times she would come within feet of deer, squirrels, rabbits, and birds. She had never explored wildlife like this before, so it was exciting for her. And she was more familiar with her surroundings now. Surprisingly enough, Rose again found the trail leading to the mansion, and this time she didn't fall. She wore boots for better traction, and her long sleeves and jeans kept her safe from pesky bugs.

When the mansion came into view, Rose briskly walked through its gates and back inside. But something was different. Rose looked down and realized that her muddy footprints were gone. "Hello? Does anyone live here?" Again there was no reply. Strange, she thought. I'm sure I tracked in mud the other day.

If anyone did live here, wouldn't they have made themselves known? Or, perhaps they were shy.

Rose sighed and continued on with her exploits. She took pictures of all the rooms and even recorded some videos. If anyone back home saw these, they would want more proof of her being here other than pictures, and selfies weren't her thing.

What she came across next was so astonishing that she nearly dropped her phone. One of Rose's favorite pastimes was reading, and she happened upon a library. The shelves were practically spilling over they were so full. Rose shoved her phone back into her pocket and reached for a book. Its cover was textured leather with black edges, and when she opened it, she saw the book was written in French. There were no pictures or drawings, so Rose had no idea what the book was about. She set it down gently and pulled another one off a shelf. This one was in English, but it might as well have been in French, for it talked about nothing other than how to play a game called battledore. Rose sat there reading for what seemed like only a few minutes, but in reality much more time had passed. She untied her washcloth and nibbled at her food as she read. When she had her fill of books, she set off for the music room.

Everything inside was just as she had left it. She sat down at the piano and played some of her favorite tunes. Some were classical, while others were modern songs played on the radio. Suddenly, she stopped in mid-song, her eyes widening as she stared down at the keys. She started to hum the same tune she heard back in the house and tried to play it on the piano. She messed up a few times, trying to find the right note to play, but she managed and quickly memorized it.

By this time the sky was turning gray as if a storm was approaching. The room darkened. She pulled her phone out to check the time. It was later than she had anticipated, and she jumped out of her chair, almost falling over. She used the flashlight on her phone to better see as the mansion was quickly darkening and she hadn't fully memorized the layout. Plus, she was alone, and that made it even worse for her; imagining unsettling things that she could run into made her skin crawl.

As she descended the stairs frantically, Rose tripped and fell to the bottom of the stairwell. She lay there for a moment, moaning as she cradled her body.

Suddenly, Rose heard footsteps behind her, but it was too dark to see. Was it an animal? Rose checked her pockets for her phone, but she dropped it when she fell. She searched the floor blindly for it, her hands shaking. When she found it, she quickly turned the flashlight back on and aimed it toward the steps.

There she saw a child crouched on the steps, holding onto the railings. "Hello there, miss."

Rose screamed and picked herself up only to fall again from the pain in her ankle. When she did regain her balance, she turned to head straight for the door only to run into another person. She almost lost her balance, but that person grabbed her wrist, and she was able to steady herself.

"Who are you?" the man demanded.

Rose could hardly make out his features. The only light besides her phone was a candle he held. "I'm sorry," she begged. "Please don't hurt me."

The man did not want an apology. He wanted her to answer his question. "Who are you, and how is it that you came to find this place? Answer me!"

Tears formed in Rose's eyes. "I'm sorry. My name is Rose. I was just walking in the forest. I'm sorry."

"Don't ever come here again! This is private property. Understand?" The man let go of her wrist, and Rose bolted for the doors. She ran with a limp and pulled the gates open, though not bothering to close them. When she looked back, the man and child were standing outside watching her.

Chapter Two

Spooked, Rose stayed clear of the mansion for the next couple of days. Of course, the idea that someone owned the place had run through her mind, but she never actually thought somebody lived there. The place was falling apart. Still, no matter what she did to keep herself occupied, the mansion was always in her thoughts.

"Rose, what do you think of this shirt?" her mother asked.

Rose and her mother were in London doing some shopping.

Rose grabbed the sleeve of the shirt to get a better look at the design. "I like it."

All the while, Rose was fascinated by the bustling life that was London. She had the opportunity to see Big Ben up close and bought a souvenir of it to take home. Her mother would force her from time to time to stand in front of a building and take photos and even asked strangers to take photos for them. Rose didn't like the attention; she preferred to blend in, but her mother was having too great of a time to stop, and by the end of the day Rose was exhausted.

Before heading back Rose and her mother stopped to have an early supper at a Chinese restaurant.

"Hey, Mom," Rose started. "What do you know about the Epping Forest?"

Tiffany finished eating her eggroll before answering. "Oh, there are stories about it being haunted and bodies being dumped there. I don't believe the stories about it being haunted, and I don't think any bodies have been found there. Why, did something happen?"

Rose shook her head. "No, I was just curious to know if there were any abandoned houses or forts there."

Tiffany shrugged. "Perhaps. Then again, I'm not the one to ask.

Maybe Diana could tell you more?"

When they returned to the house, Rose's father was watching TV, and she could smell that he had made himself something to eat, so she didn't feel bad eating without him.

"What's all this?" Luke asked after seeing all their shopping bags. "Did you two buy all of London?"

Tiffany laughed. "Just about," she said. "We had a great time. You should have come with us."

Luke shook his head. "And get caught carrying all of your bags? I don't think so."

"I'll be upstairs putting my things away." Rose said, already heading up the stairs.

She dumped her bags in a corner and started pulling out her purchases and putting them in the dresser.

When Rose was done sorting through everything she bought, she headed up to the attic to look through the remaining crates and paintings and anything else that was there. A cool breeze was still blowing through the cracked window, and it had pushed off more sheets.

Propped against a wall were stacks of paintings like the one she saw earlier. Each was a painting of a family: a father, mother and their daughter. Rose was careful not to touch the artwork and held it by its frame so as not to damage it from the oils on her fingers. She carefully set each painting aside and soon discovered each was a painting of the same family. On the last painting she noticed a date: 1783. Curious, Rose brought the painting downstairs to show her parents and maybe get some answers.

Luke and Tiffany were sitting the living room watching a show when they saw Rose from the corner of their eyes standing in the doorway.

Tiffany immediately muted the TV and asked, "Where did you find that?"

Rose motioned with her head toward the stairs. "In the attic," she told them. "I've found other things like sheet music, letters, and books." She paused. "There are more paintings up there, too."

"You should put it back," Luke cautioned.

Rose rolled her eyes. "I'm not going to break it. I'm being extra careful, I swear. I just want to know if you could tell me anything about the woman in the painting. There are a few more of her up in the attic." Rose was genuinely curious and didn't mean to upset her parents.

Tiffany finally spoke up. "I'm not sure we're the right people to ask. Maybe Diana and Alan know? They've owned the property for years." She pulled out her phone and snapped a picture of the painting. "I'll show Diana this when I see her next and ask for you."

Rose nodded. "Thanks, Mom." She knew there was a good chance her parents wouldn't know anything, but it hadn't hurt to ask. Rose had the feeling Diana or Alan wouldn't know either.

Rose placed the painting back in the attic along with the rest of the paintings and put the sheet back over it. That was not the end of Rose's excursion. She opened another crate and rummaged through it. There were simply too many letters to read, and the light outside was fading fast, so she carried the crate down to her room.

There was a bundle of letters bound by a thick string. Rose struggled to get the knot open. She could have easily snipped the string, but she didn't want to ruin even that and managed to get the knot out after a few moments. The letters were wrapped in a thin white handkerchief, which Rose gently unfolded.

Propped on her bed, Rose started reading the letters:

My dearest Elizabeth,

I hope you enjoyed the dinner and dance. When spring comes around, I want to host another one. I pray that you will be able to make it;

it was a joy to have you there. I can only hope that it was the same for you. Also, I wanted to know what you thought…

The words were no longer visible, so Rose picked up another letter to read.

My dearest Elizabeth,

I have heard word that you are very ill. I pray that your good health returns soon. In a month I shall come see you. Don't worry, I will be there to take care of you just as you have done for me in the past…

Again the letter stopped. The rest of the writing seemed to have been washed away.

Many of the letters were like this. Rose wrapped them back up before replacing them into the crate. Looking out the window, she watched as the sun disappeared beyond the horizon, setting off shadows in the forest. And there standing was the little boy she had seen when she first wandered into the forest. He was holding a small red box, which he slowly set down on the ground before running away from view.

At first Rose hesitated to go and look what was in the box. Was it left for her? Her curiosity got the better of her, and she sneaked downstairs and out the back door. She didn't want her parents asking what she was doing or where she was going.

Before picking up the box, Rose looked around to see if she could see the boy, but he was gone. Not wanting bugs to crawl inside it, Rose picked up the box and dashed back to her room.

The exterior of the box was covered in velvet and the inside with black silk. Placed inside was a tiny, rolled-up piece of paper. The handwriting was exquisite. The letter read:

Greetings Miss,

Please do not be alarmed. My master and I are kind people; we were just overwhelmed by your appearance. As you might have guessed, we were not expecting visitors. I hope that you can forgive us for scaring you so. After giving it much thought, we would like to welcome you back to the mansion. I do hope you accept this invitation, but I will not blame you if you decide not to join us for tea tomorrow afternoon.

Sincerely, T.A.

Rose scoffed, ready to rip the letter in half, but stopped and placed it back inside the box, which she then set it on her nightstand as a reminder. She would sleep on the idea of whether or not she would accept the invitation.

For the next couple of days, Rose let the box sit on the nightstand. It was a constant reminder of what she encountered at the mansion. It was almost torturous for her, but something told her to keep it and not say a word to her parents. Perhaps the thought would just go away and she could move on, but as another day passed, the thought remained.

Diana did know something about the young lady in the painting. The contents of the attic had remained untouched since before she and Alan took control of the house. There was little known about it other than it was built in the early eighteenth century. The lady in the painting had to have been one of its first residents. But that little bit of information was hardly satisfying for Rose.

She still badly wanted to accept the invitation to tea, despite several days having passed. Her parents were away for the day, and she was tempted to return to the mansion. But what if she did, and the people there wouldn't let her leave? She couldn't help but have those thoughts. If she didn't come back by the end of the day, though, she knew her parents would go looking for her.

Thus, it was decided: Rose got dressed for the day and grabbed her shoulder bag, placing inside it her phone, the box, and some sheet music she had found in one of the crates. She thought that maybe she could play the piano for them as a thank you and to show she meant no trouble. As usual, she left her parents a note.

It took Rose thirty minutes to reach the mansion. As she stood outside its gates, a gust of wind pushed her forward as if telling her to go in. The front yard was as quiet as ever. There were no birds chirping or insects singing, only the sound of her boots crushing the dirt and grass beneath underfoot. Before Rose could knock, the doors slowly opened and standing there was the boy. He had short, curly brown hair and brown eyes and wore a loose-fitting white cotton shirt with simple brown trousers and brown boots. His clothes looked dated, but Rose tried not to pay any mind to it.

He was surprised to see her and smiled. "Oh, hello there, miss. I was not expecting to ever see you again." He stepped to the side. "I was just on my way into the forest, but that can wait. Please, come inside."

Stepping into the mansion was different this time. It no longer felt forbidden or deserted.

"Follow me, if you will." The boy took the lead and motioned to Rose to follow him.

Rose was taken aback by his manners. She had never met a child of his age, or any age, who spoke so formally. As she continued behind him, he led her to a place she had not been before: the dining room. Curtains were spread open, leaving the room so bright the light almost blinded her. It took a few seconds for her eyes to adjust, and when they did, she saw a stunning, long table made completely out of glass. A thin, white tablecloth lay over it, and a tea set was placed in perfect order on the far end in front of three wooden chairs painted white.

"Please, take a seat and make yourself at home," the boy said, pulling out a chair for Rose to sit in. "By the way, my name is Thackeray, Thackeray Ashton. I will be back shortly, I promise."

"Oh, my name is Rose Fair."

27

Thackeray smiled. "Nice to meet you, Rose." He grabbed the tea pot and left the room.

As Rose sat in silence, she hung her shoulder bag on the chairback and folded her hands, taking in her surroundings. The dining room was spotless, not a fingerprint on anything. Suddenly, she checked her boots to see if they were clean, not wanting to track in mud again. Thankfully, there was no dirt or mud to be found, and she was able to relax. She laughed to herself for being there and glanced out the windows, only to see trees. As far as Rose could tell, the forest went on for miles.

The door to the dining room opened, and Rose sat up straight, her heart racing. A tall, pale, blond man walked in. He wore a white cotton tunic with ruffles around the neck and cuffs, perfectly fitting black breeches, and scruffy black leather riding boots. His long hair was tied back with a black ribbon. He sat down across the table from Rose, his strong jawline, nose, and broad shoulders making him look even more intimidating. But it was his kind, hazel eyes that set Rose at ease. He must be in his early twenties at least, Rose thought.

"I believe you are Miss Rose, am I correct?"

Rose nodded.

The man cleared his throat. "I must apologize for how I treated you last time. Allow me to formally introduce myself." He cleared his throat again. He must have been just as nervous as Rose. "My name is Edmond Valcain."

Thackeray returned at that moment with a silver tray. On it was a tea pot and a plate of scones with berries. He set it down carefully and poured each of them a cup of tea. He placed a scone on a smaller plate and set it in front of Rose. "I hope you like scones," he said.

"I've never had one," she replied. Rose had seen them on menus but had never ordered one. She took a bite and chewed slowly. "It's good," she finally said and took another bite.

Thackeray smiled and blew on his tea.

"We don't get very many visitors," Edmond said, never taking his eyes off Rose.

"I noticed," she said as she blew on her tea.

Edmond ignored her comment. "We try to keep this place in good form as best as we can."

Rose finally took a sip of her tea. It was good. "So, are you guys part of a re-enactment?" she asked, eyeing their clothing.

Edmond looked confused. "I beg your pardon?"

Rose set her tea down. "Your clothes," she said. "Are you and Thackeray part of a re-enactment? Like role-playing the past?"

Edmond looked down at his shirt and felt it with his hands. "No, these are my regular clothes," he said earnestly. "I was just about to ask you about your clothes. I've never seen a woman wear pants."

Rose raised a brow. "Are you serious?"

Edmond didn't answer. "You're definitely not British or Irish or German. Where do you come from?"

Rose couldn't help but laugh, but when she saw the mortified look on his face, she stopped and cleared her throat. She looked over at Thackeray, who just shrugged. He had no idea where she was from either. Finally, she answered them. "I'm from America."

"So that's what Americans sound like," Edmond said, looking at Thackeray.

"Am I honestly the first American you have met?" Rose asked.

Thackeray was quick to respond. "We don't get out much."

Rose refrained from rolling her eyes. "Clearly," and took a sip of her tea. "Oh, I just remembered." She set her cup down and grabbed her shoulder bag. When she couldn't find the red box, she took out the sheets of music and set it on the table. "Ah-ha!" she exclaimed, spotting the box. "I believe this is yours," and handed it to Thackeray.

Edmond reached over and grabbed the sheets of music and looked them over. "Do you play?"

Rose nodded. "I do. My mom is a music teacher, and she taught me how to play the piano."

Edmond handed back the music. "Would you like to play the piano?"

"Right now?" Rose asked.

"If you want to," he said. "But we can finish out tea first."

When they finished their tea, the three of them walked to the music room. The place looked different with the sun shining in.

Rose sat down and started to play.

Hearing the music, Thackeray began dancing around the room, while Edmond stood next to the piano with his arm resting on top of it. The music made even Rose want to dance.

When it was over, Edmond asked, "Where did you find this music?"

"In a crate in the attic at the house I'm staying in for the summer," Rose said. "I found a lot of things."

"Is it the house about a mile west from here?" Edmond asked.

Rose nodded. "Yeah, how did you know?"

Edmond waved his hand dismissively. "I've come across it a few times." He picked up another piece of music and handed it to Rose. "Will you play another song?"

Rose started playing again, though she didn't believe he was telling the whole truth. This time, the song was somber, and Thackeray stopped dancing and took a seat on a nearby couch. Rose soon noticed from the corner of her eye that Edmond was following along perfectly. "You know the song," Rose said, looking up at Edmond.

Taken aback, Edmond replied, "What do you mean?"

"I mean exactly what I say." She wasn't trying to be rude; she just wanted to know why Edmond was being evasive.

Thackeray slid onto the piano bench next to Rose and asked, "Will you teach me how to play?"

Rose knew it was a diversion, but she smiled at Thackeray and nodded. "Place your hands here." Thackeray mimicked her.

Edmond walked toward the piano, then turned to face the two and said: "I must apologize. There is something important that I forgot to do. Please, continue without me."

"Where are you going?" asked Rose.

Edmond smiled and gave her a small bow. "That, Rose, is a secret." And he left the room.

After Edmond left the room, he quietly closed the door behind himself and leaned on it. He sighed, smiling. It had been many years since someone played those songs in this mansion. In a way Rose reminded him of her—yes, her, his beloved. And hearing those two play the piano gave him hope for the future.

He started up the staircase and down the hall and through one of the doors until he reached another flight of stairs and made his way into the attic. The door squeaked as he opened it, and he came upon a comfortable lounging area. You wouldn't think it an attic with its blankets and comfy cushions lying around. Under a window was a small table with painting tools on top of it.

Next to the table was an easel covered by a white sheet. Edmond gripped it, as if to pull it off, but he stopped, unable to do it. It was a long while before Edmond finally removed the sheet, letting it fall to his feet. Dust flew up and around him, but he didn't seem bothered by it.

The oil-based painting on canvas was of a young woman. Her bare

31

back was facing the eyes of the painter; her long, wavy blond hair pulled to one side. Her head was slightly turned as she glanced over her uncovered shoulder. Her blue eyes dazzled above her soft pink cheeks and lustrous red lips.

Edmond looked at the painting with both desire and pain in his eyes. He knew this young woman well. And as he whispered her name, he felt as if he was being betrayed. "Elizabeth."

Rose finished playing the last piece of music and looked at the time on her phone. "I should be getting back," she said. "If my parents are home and I'm gone for too long, they'll start to worry."

"It feels like you only just got here," Thackeray said, looking sad. "Will you come back tomorrow? I'll make more tea and scones for us." He sounded hopeful.

Rose smiled at him. "I will try," she said with sincerity. "Do you know where Edmond went off to? I'd like to say goodbye to him. And what was so important?"

Thackeray rubbed his chin. "Edmond is full of many secrets. You'll have to forgive my master."

Rose gave him an odd look. "Why do you call him 'master'?"

Thackeray continued to stroke his chin. "A long time ago Edmond took me in from off the streets. He had a school here once, but...."

"Enough, Thackeray," said Edmond, standing at the doorway. "Rose is right. Her parents might start to worry, and we don't want that." His face softened. "Thank you for coming, Rose. Come again tomorrow, if you wish."

Rose couldn't help but think it all too weird. First the clothes, then the formal talking, and them not having a clue as to where she came from, and the fact that Thackeray called Edmond "master" was just all very weird to her. "You're right," started Rose. "My parents will want me home." She then stopped to think: home, that was back in California. Rose quickly gathered her belongings and said her goodbyes.

Edmond and Thackeray watched in silence as she left, and when she was out of sight, Thackeray looked at Edmond. "I'm sorry. Please forgive me."

Edmond huffed. "Sorry isn't good enough. Rose must never find out the truth about us."

Thackeray couldn't help but defend himself on this subject. "If you don't want her to find out about us, then why did you have me send for her?" Before he even finished his sentence, he regretted saying it, but he couldn't help it. He stepped back quickly, thinking Edmond would raise a hand at him, but he did not.

Edmond started to explain himself. "She reminds me of her; her music and the way she carries herself. It's almost too good to be true, don't you think?"

Thackeray leaned against the wall, his arms crossed. "Sure, she does, but is it wise to have her come back? Why risk our secret?"

Edmond thought as he took a seat on the couch. "How long has it been since we've had a visitor, Thackeray?" Edmond knew the answer, but he wanted to hear it from Thackeray.

"Far too long, master," he said with a smile and joined Edmond on the couch. "What if she finds out?"

Edmond's face softened. "If she is fit to learn our secret, we will know well before she finds out."

Thackeray laughed. "This is very unlike you. Are you sure you're feeling well?"

Edmond leaned back on the couch and rested his arms behind his head. "Thackeray, my dear old friend, I haven't felt this well in a very long time."

That night as Rose lay in bed, after a hearty supper with her parents, she thought back on her day with Edmond and Thackeray. They seemed nice for the most part, but the way they dressed and spoke puzzled her. Were they runaways? No. Did Edmond kidnap Thackeray, and now they were hiding out in the mansion? The idea was plausible, and perhaps that was why Edmond didn't want her there at first. Then again, if that was the case, surely Thackeray would have said something. Rose tried not to give it much thought; she didn't want to freak herself out. She was already surprised that she went there in the first place.

Tired and frustrated with herself, she rubbed her eyes and pulled the covers over her head. If she was going to continue to go back there, she wanted to get some answers, and she would do it all by herself if she had to.

Chapter Three

It was early morning as Thackeray sat on a wooden stool watching Edmond organize plants in the garden.

Edmond kneeled as he clipped off purple stems, squeezing the juice from them and pouring it into a bottle filled with a blue liquid. Next, he took the red leaves from the same flowers and crushed them on a cutting board, putting them into the same bottle. The leaves slowly dissolved and turned the blue liquid dark green. The only things left from the flowers were the red buds.

Curious, Thackeray asked, "Why are you making another potion?"

Edmond said nothing.

Thackeray sighed. "You have plenty left from the last time you made some." He paused, hoping Edmond would say something, but he didn't. "It's not like either of us need it anymore."

"An old habit, I guess," Edmond finally offered, still working on the potion.

Thackeray, suddenly worried, sat up a little straighter. "You wouldn't dare."

"Dare what?" Edmond stopped what he was doing to look up at his friend.

Thackeray pointed at the potion. "Are you going to try to make Rose drink it?"

Edmond was surprised Thackeray would think such a thought, and an offended look washed over his face. "Of course not."

"Then why are you making that potion? You haven't made it in years."

Beside himself, Edmond let out an exasperated sigh. "Like I said, old habit. Other than that, I haven't the faintest idea why."

Thackeray slipped off his stool and knelt beside Edmond. "If you're worried about Rose, don't be. Everything will be fine."

Edmond looked over at his friend and said: "It is strange hearing you speak that way. I'm used to seeing a little boy, and at times I forget that you are much older than that."

Later that day, Rose was at the local library with her father. Her mother was out with Diana and other friends, so today it was just them. Rose took this opportunity to get information on the mansion and headed straight for the computers. She looked up various haunted mansions in England but found nothing that resembled the mansion she had stumbled upon. She even looked up Epping Forest.

She next searched for anything about the last name Valcain. The only thing that showed up was information on where the name originated and what it meant. That told Rose little except it originated in another part of England and was not to be found elsewhere in Europe. At least Edmond was truthful about his name.

Rose then looked up Thackeray's last name, Ashton. That search yielded hundreds of family trees and places from which the families had started out. It was clear that Thackeray's last name had more records, but when it came to the boy himself, Rose found nothing. Searching for Edmond's background proved just as futile. Rose sighed and sat back in her chair. There had to be a better way of finding out about the mansion.

If there was a way to find out about something historical—or, according to Rose, ancient—there was only one way to do it: by looking up old records and books. She walked up to a librarian and asked to see the oldest books in the library.

The librarian thought for a moment, then said: "This way. I'll show you."

After passing a small art gallery in the basement, they continued to a back room that smelled of musty old books. "I hope you find what you're looking for," said the librarian before leaving Rose to help someone else.

The room was filled with filing cabinets. Everything was in alphabetical order, but when Rose went down the list, she found nothing about the mansion, Edmond, or Thackeray. It was as if they were ghosts, forgotten by history itself. Rose laughed at the thought. "They aren't ghosts," she told herself. "Ghosts can't drink tea."

Exasperated, she thought the best thing for her to do was to ask Edmond or Thackeray upfront. But could she trust them? They acted as if they had never before seen another human being.

Rose stomped her foot out of frustration and heard something slide behind one of the bookshelves. She walked to where she heard the noise and tried to peer into the space between the wall and the shelf. There was definitely something stuck there. At first, she tried to grab it by forcing her hand into the space, but she almost got stuck.

The shelf was too heavy for her to move, so she took off her belt and slid it between the wall and the shelf, trying to latch it onto whatever the object was. After several attempts she succeeded, and a thin book dropped at her feet.

A thick layer of dust covered the book, so Rose used the sleeve of her shirt to clean it off. She gasped at what she saw. The title read "Epping Massacre."

Rose opened the book and started to read. The book talked about black magic and witchcraft and a giant fire that nearly took down Epping Forest. It mentioned a young lord of a mansion who practiced with said magic and the school he had established in his home to teach young boys, and even some girls, the art of witchcraft.

There were detailed drawings and descriptions of what had occurred.

Rose found it hard to continue because some of the drawings were of children being burned alive or bludgeoned to death.

Just as she could stand no more, she turned a page to find a horrific drawing of a man. His blond hair was long and snarled, his eyes crazed, and his smile haunting.

Rose nearly dropped the book when she heard her father call out to her. He was standing in the doorway.

"Are you ready to go?" he asked.

Rose nodded. "Yeah, I'll be right there." She waited until he was out of sight before stuffing the book into her bag. No one would miss it. It must have been wedged behind the shelf for decades.

When they arrived back at the house, Tiffany was still gone with Diana.

"It looks like we're on our own for lunch," Luke said with a sigh. "What do you want to eat?"

Rose thought for a moment. "Nothing too fancy; maybe some sandwiches or pasta?"

Luke nodded. "I like the idea of pasta. I'll get some water boiling. Do you want to make the sauce?"

Rose's answer was left hanging in the air as she thought: "Let me wash up really quickly. That library was filled with so many dusty books. Honestly, do people not read books anymore?" she thought out loud, only half joking. She mainly wanted to go upstairs to read more of the book she had taken from the library.

"Don't take too long," Luke said as he headed into the kitchen.

Rose didn't bother washing up. She planned to return to the mansion to ask Edmond about the book she had found. She plopped onto her bed, took the book out of her bag, and quickly found the spot where she had left off.

The book told gruesome tales of black magic and witchcraft and what was done to people. The author even mentioned how terrified he was for even writing the book. This was not something meant for those outside the small circle of followers.

Rose continued on, reading about the lord of the mansion. She learned that he fought back with the help the children and servants, and even his lover. But try they did and they failed. The lord poisoned himself, along with his lover, and their bodies were burned with the rest of the household's. But who were these people? The book never said. No names were mentioned.

The last few pages were blank, and Rose, unsure what to think, closed the book with a sigh. Was it true, or was it just meant to scare children into staying in their beds at night.

Rose returned the book to her bag and headed downstairs to have supper, only to find her father snoring on the couch. Chuckling, she turned off the burner on the stove, left a note for him, and headed to the mansion.

The evening seemed more humid than usual, and Rose was bombarded by ladybugs, flies, and other pesky bugs as she walked toward the mansion. When she arrived, she knocked on the front doors and waited before knocking again. Finally, she let herself in. "Hello, is anybody home? Thackeray? Edmond?"

Neither seemed to be around as Rose looked in all the rooms she had previously been in.

Then, she heard giggling and followed the sound to a back door. With one good push, she opened the door and stood there flabbergasted. The ground was littered with tiny flowers of all colors and shapes. The trees were well tended and the bushes were neatly trim, unlike in the forest. A brick wall was covered with roses and other climbing flowers. The whole back yard was a giant fairytale garden. Without a doubt, Edmond and Thackeray spent most of their time out there making it beautiful.

Thackeray popped out from behind one of the trees chasing a butterfly. When he saw Rose, he stopped, letting the butterfly get away. "Rose!" he called out. "You came back!" By the time he reached her, he was nearly out of breath. His face flushed a pale pink, and he quickly looked away when he saw Rose in a tank top. Thackeray had never seen a girl show so much skin. "I was afraid we might have scared you off," he said. Finally, he forced himself to look back at her so as not to seem rude.

"Yeah, I'm sorry about that. I got held up. I went to the library with my dad today."

Thackeray smiled. "It's all right. You're here now, and that's all that matters."

"Rose?" asked a voice from behind.

Rose turned to see Edmond. His hair was tied back again, and his hands were stained with dirt. She also noticed that he was wearing the same clothes from the other day although now they were covered in dirt and grass.

Edmond, too, had noticed her tank top and was just as surprised as Thackeray had been. "I didn't think you would be here today," Edmond said.

"Yeah, I was with my dad at the library." She suddenly remembered the book. "Oh, before I forget, I found this. I was wondering if you could tell me anything about it."

She took the book from her bag and handed it to Edmond. "The Epping Massacre," he read aloud, raising a brow. "What about it?" He handed the book back to her.

"I thought maybe you would know something about it since it happened in this forest," Rose said.

"I'm sorry," Edmond said with an apologetic grin. "I'm afraid I don't know anything about this."

Rose frowned, hoping to get something—anything—out of him.

"The back yard looks amazing," she said as she took another look around.

"Thank you," said Edmond. "Thackeray and I take great pride in taking care of it. We enjoy our outdoor activities." He paused. "Do you like outdoor activities, Rose?"

"Depends on the activity."

A mischievous grin appeared on Edmond's face. "Do you play croquet?"

Rose had heard of the game but couldn't remember anything about it. "I've never played it."

Edmond was eager to show her how. "Luckily for you, Rose, Thackeray and I know how to play." He snapped his fingers to get Thackeray's attention. "Go get the equipment, will you? We're going to show Rose how to play."

Thackeray jumped up and down with excitement. "I'll be back as soon as I can." He dashed past them and went inside the manor, leaving Edmond and Rose alone.

As they waited, Rose flipped through the pages of the book again, seeing if she had missed anything.

Edmond finally spoke up, breaking the silence. "So, you say you're from America, yes? Where at?" he asked.

"California," she told him. "It's a very long way from here. I thought I was going to die on the way over here," recalling her cramped seat on the plane.

"California?" Edmond repeated. "I've never heard of it. It sounds like a great place, though."

Rose refrained from giving him another odd look. "What about you? Where in England are you originally from?"

Edmond tried to rub the dirt from his hands. "I've always lived here."

Rose nodded. "Oh, I see. So, you're from Loughton?"

"More or less," he said. "I've always lived in this mansion."

Rose put the book back in her bag. "But the mansion is so old."

Edmond could not deny that. "It is, but it's a good home. I was born and raised in this mansion, so it's hard to let go."

Rose was confused. "What do you mean?"

Edmond looked behind himself to see if Thackeray had returned, then looked back at Rose. "Long story short: my mother died giving birth to me, and when I was twelve, my father passed away from a fever. Ever since then I have been in charge of the mansion."

Rose was sorry to hear about his mother, but what came out of her mouth was not an apology. "Now I know you're pulling my leg."

Now Edmond was the confused one. "I…I think not," he told her, as he was clearly not touching her leg.

"I meant you're joking." Rose explained.

Edmond wasn't sure what to tell her. He was not looking to tell a joke. "No. I'm telling you the truth. You don't believe me?"

Rose felt insulted. "Well, of course I don't. You expect me to believe a mansion was left in the hands of a twelve year old?"

Edmond sighed. "Let's not fight," he said. "Let's try to enjoy ourselves."

"You're right. I'm sorry."

"No. It's my fault entirely," Edmond said quickly.

Rose definitely wasn't going to fight him on this one. "If you say so."

Thackeray's voice echoed across the yard as he returned, and he handed Rose and Edmond each a mallet. He then set up the rest of the game.

"Follow me," said Edmond. As Rose followed alongside him, he patiently explained the rules and showed her how to hit the ball and where it was supposed to go. After a few practice turns, the real game began.

Rose stomped her foot as the ball bounced off the metal wicket and failed to go through the hoop.

Edmond couldn't help but laugh. "Be patient," he said. "Take your time."

Rose wanted to pick up the ball and throw it at him. "I am being patient," she fired back.

This only made Edmond laugh at her more. "You are so strange." He walked over to her and slowly wrapped his arms around her. "Here, let me help you." Rose didn't have time to protest as Edmond was already taking full control of her mallet. "Now look closely and keep both eyes open. If you squint, you will do yourself no good." He pulled the mallet back gently. "Each mallet is different. You must examine it to see which side is smoother." He quickly flipped the mallet. "And gently hit the ball. Sometimes all you need is a little nudge. If you want to get better, leave out the fancy tricks and stick with basics."

"I know this," Rose said, flushing a pale pink.

Edmond struck the ball, and all three watched as it went through the hoop.

"Yes!" Rose shot her arms in the air, accidently hitting Edmond in the face. Rose spun around quickly, dropping the mallet, and put her hands to her mouth. "Oh, I'm sorry. Are you okay?"

Edmond staggered back a few feet, holding his nose. "I'll be fine."

Thackeray pulled a handkerchief from his pants pocket and handed it to Edmond.

"Thank you, Thackeray." Edmond brought the handkerchief to his nose to plug the bleeding.

Rose continued to apologize until Edmond put up a hand to stop her.

"It's fine, really. You didn't mean to," he said as droplets of blood escaped the fold of the handkerchief and fell onto his shirt.

Rose frowned. "Oh no, your shirt is ruined."

"All I need is a wet cloth. Everything is fine, Rose." Edmond wished she would stop blaming herself. It was nothing serious, he assured her, and his shirt was dirty to begin with.

"Let's head inside and get cleaned up, shall we?" Thackeray suggested. "I'll make us some more tea. How does that sound?"

"That sounds wonderful, Thackeray," Edmond said, and the three of them headed inside.

Rose and Edmond sat in the music room while Thackeray prepared a tray of tea.

"I really am sorry about your nose," Rose said, feeling it was necessary to apologize one last time as she sipped her tea. "What can I do to make it up to you?"

Edmond pointed at the piano. "Play something for me."

Rose was more than happy to play something for Edmond. She immediately started to play a joyful, energetic song that prompted Thackeray to get up from his seat, dancing and singing.

"Just like old times, huh, Thackeray?" Edmond said.

Thackeray smiled. "I remember," he said. "And do you remember when we would spend days like this with Elizabeth? It was the best!"

Edmond smiled back. "Indeed, they were."

Rose abruptly stopped playing, and Thackeray and Edmond turned to look at her.

"Why did you stop?" Thackeray asked.

Rose could only stare at the keyboard, deep in thought. "Elizabeth,"

44

she finally said, remembering all those old letters.

Thackeray and Edmond glanced at each other and then looked back at Rose.

"What was Elizabeth like?" she asked.

Edmond was taken aback by her question. "That's a sensitive subject."

Rose stood up from the chair and started gathering her things.

"Where are you going?" asked Thackeray.

"I'm leaving," she said bluntly.

"Will you be back tomorrow?" Thackeray asked, looking hopeful.

Rose sighed. "I don't think so. I've spent too much time here as it is, and I should be getting back now. My dad is probably awake from his nap."

"Did we do something to upset you?" Thackeray wanted to know.

Rose tried to explain. "Look, I hardly know you, and it's fair that you don't want to tell me certain things, but I thought it was strange that you didn't know where my accent came from or why you wear the clothes that you do." Then, thinking aloud: "Is this some kind of reality show and there are hidden cameras everywhere? Am I the joke of the show?"

Edmond and Thackeray looked confused. "Show? Joke?" Edmond said. "We haven't told you any jokes, Rose, and we're not showing anything."

An awkward silence befell the room. No one said anything for a long while, and Rose was finding it difficult to move her feet and leave. Suddenly, she found herself asking, "Are you two ghosts, or time travelers?"

Thackeray and Edmond looked at each other. In the end it was Thackeray who spoke up. "In a way we are time travelers, but not in the way you're thinking."

Rose, not knowing how to respond, remained silent.

"We're certainly not ghosts," added Edmond. "I'm afraid it is more complicated than that."

Rose took a seat by the piano. "Go on," she told him.

Edmond cleared his throat before continuing: "The girl you ask about, Elizabeth, she wrote those songs you brought with you. She was smart, loved to sing and dance, and was a master at playing the piano. Elizabeth was also my wife." He struggled to get out that last sentence, Rose could tell. "The book you showed me, the massacre did happen. It's all real, except for the black magic and witchcraft. That was entirely made up by the minds of sick people."

Thackeray's mouth dropped. "I thought you didn't want to tell her."

Edmond put up a hand to silence him. "It is true," he said. "All of it is. That's why for many years we have stayed here protecting this mansion, and if anyone gets close, we scare them off. You're the first we've ever thought about letting come back."

Rose wrapped her arms around herself as if frozen in place. "Who exactly are you people?"

"We're exactly who we say we are. We are just like you, Rose; only time has stopped for us," Thackeray said.

"Stopped?" Rose asked, shooting a puzzled look at Edmond. "I think it's time you tell me this big secret of yours; otherwise, I'm never going to understand."

He took a deep breath. "Perhaps it is time, but if you were Thackeray or me, you would understand."

"Then tell me. Help me understand," she implored. "I want you to tell me everything."

"Everything," Edmond said, adjusting himself in the chair before continuing. "What I am about to tell you, Rose, you may or may not

46

believe. All I ask is that you keep this to yourself. You must never tell a single soul. Do you understand?"

Rose nodded.

"Good," said Edmond. "Then I hope you still think of me as human once I'm done telling you."

Thackeray sat cross-legged on the floor, like a child getting ready for storytime. Only, Thackeray knew this story well, for he had lived it.

"1785 was the year it happened. I was twenty-two," began Edmond. "As I have told you before, I came into control of this mansion at the age of twelve, when my parents died. I was known as "The Master" back in those days. I must admit I was rude and conceited, but I was still good to those who served me." He paused, trying to remember how the pieces of his story all fit together. "I met Elizabeth when I was thirteen. It's because of her that I turned my rude ways around. She was smart and funny, and she didn't care if she was inappropriate. Elizabeth was always herself, and I adored that about her. She made me laugh more than anyone else.

"As time went on, Elizabeth and I fell in love, but she was betrothed to someone else...as luck would have it." He chuckled sadly. "I think his name was Viktor Slater. Elizabeth didn't really know him, and she was too innocent to see him for the man he really was. Nonetheless, Elizabeth agreed to marry him in order to make her parents happy. She did try to protest, but her parents never allowed it."

Rose spoke up. "Why didn't she tell her parents that she loved you?"

Edmond sighed. "Her parents didn't think much about me. I begged Elizabeth to call off the engagement, but she was scared."

Rose looked at him with sympathy.

"Please," Edmond said, "do not feel sorry for me. In the end what I made Elizabeth go through is unforgivable." And then he added quietly: "I wanted to keep her forever for my own selfish reasons. I loved her too much to the point that I couldn't let her go."

Thackeray huffed. "Don't say such things! What Elizabeth did was of her own free will. The choice was hers alone."

Edmond just shook his head and went on with his story. "So, the time came when I was to marry. I turned away so many fine young women, for the only woman I wanted was Elizabeth. I realized at that moment that I didn't have the time to be choosy. I needed a wife to carry on my legacy. And then one day, as Thackeray and I were hunting, we came across a peculiar flower. We had never seen anything like it."

Thackeray interjected, "The flowers are still out there, if you look hard enough."

Edmond waited for Thackeray to finish speaking, then continued: "At the same time people in the local area were getting deathly ill. I wanted to find a way to help them. So, I took the flowers—Thackeray and I—and we studied them. We first tried them out with other plants, mixing them with various herbs and liquids and testing them on sick animals."

"What happened to them?" Rose asked.

Edmond seemed pleased that she asked. "The animals healed within a day or two. And then the day came when a servant of mine, a young girl —Lora I think her name was— fell ill with a fever, and I tried the potion I had made with the flower on her. Her fever died down within a few hours, and she was well again."

Rose was impressed. "That's amazing."

Edmond continued. "And then the night came when I fell terribly sick with the flu. My fever was rising, and I couldn't keep down even water. I was dying."

Rose cut in. "You used the potion on yourself?"

Edmond nodded. "But just one sip, one vial, was not enough. I was still dying, and I thought surely that was the end for me. So, in my state of terror, if I was going to die anyway, I drank all the potions I had."

"Ten potions total," Thackeray said. "I know this because I helped him make them."

"As the night went on," Edmond continued. "I fell asleep, and when I awoke late the next morning, I was a new person. I had this energy I'd never had before, this strength that made me feel invincible."

Curious, Rose asked: "What kind of potion was this? Did it make you immortal?"

"This may sound crazy, but the potion slowed down your age until it stopped altogether," Edmond replied. "But here was the catch: the potion only kept you alive if you stayed in the area, meaning the forest. It's something in the air, Rose. A toxin the flowers give off. So, if you were to venture too far out, you would start to age and turn to dust, but only if you had lived passed a normal life expectancy. For example, if you drank the potion now, in a hundred years, if you traveled passed the forest, your body would start to age until you became nothing but dust."

"How do you know all this?" Rose asked, but when she saw the pained look on Edmond's face, she reconsidered finding out. "Never mind, you don't have to tell me."

Edmond went on with his story. "After a few months word got out that I was using black magic and witchcraft. People were saying that I was teaching children the art of the devil and damned me to hell. In the end it didn't matter what I tried telling the people; they had made up their minds long ago about me.

"And then one winter night they came to get us. Elizabeth was there with me. The weather was poor, and I didn't want to risk having her get sick. I remember seeing their torches in the distance. It was frightening." He closed his eyes for a moment, recalling the past. "I still remember everything Elizabeth said to me that night."

Rose listened attentively, picturing everything Edmond said as if she had been there watching it all happen.

The shouting of the villagers could be heard from outside the mansion. Elizabeth held on tight to Edmond, her whole body paralyzed by terror. "Edmond, please don't leave me," she begged.

"I would never leave you," said Edmond and kissed her softly on the lips. He took her hand then, and together they ran through the mansion, trying to find a safe way out. They could hear the banging on the front doors and the people cursing their names. Edmond tried to shield Elizabeth from all of that and led her into the kitchen where most of the screaming and yelling was muffled. He broke open a floorboard and pulled out a metal box.

Inside lay three large vials of the potion. Picking one up, Edmond handed it to Elizabeth. "Drink this," he urged.

Elizabeth was crying now. "I can't."

Edmond caressed Elizabeth's cheek. "Elizabeth," he said, "if you want to be together, you must drink this, but if you don't, I will not be angry. Listen to me carefully, though; if those people find you, they may very well kill you. But if you drink this, there is a good chance your life will be spared."

"What about the others?" she asked.

The entrance to the mansion was finally broken down, and the real horror began. Screams of innocents could be heard echoing from all parts of the mansion.

"Now or never, Elizabeth!" Edmond said in haste.

Without another second to spare, Elizabeth opened the vial and swallowed the potion in one gulp. "It's horrible," she said, grimacing.

Edmond handed Elizabeth the box and said: "Drink the rest. You may pass out from it, but at least the villagers will think you poisoned yourself." He kissed her forehead. "I have to go help the others now."

Rose was almost in tears. Edmond's story was breaking her heart. Was it all true? Was Edmond really from the eighteenth century?

"As I left her, it broke my heart," said Edmond. "I left her with a box of potions, and by the time I found the others, it was too late. I quickly grabbed a rapier next to the fireplace there in the great room, and when I turned around, I saw one of the boys I used to teach. His shirt was covered in blood, and his face turning gray. I held him until he died; it was all I could do for him. And in my rage I went after the villagers and fought them.

"I yelled and cursed at them, telling them to come after me instead. That was the first and only time I ever took another human being's life. Their numbers were too great, and they overpowered me. They knocked me unconscious, thinking I would die. The mansion was on fire, but the snow that fell that night put it out.

"When I woke up the next morning, all of my wounds were healed. Corpses of my students and servants were everywhere. Elizabeth, Thackeray and I were the only survivors. Sadly, Elizabeth could never return home. She heard word that her parents had left the house they were living in, the one you are staying in now, and they were never heard from again. Perhaps they were sick with grief, or perhaps they were ashamed of their daughter, I don't know. Sometimes I think she would have been better off never knowing me, but who is to say?" He paused for a moment. "That is the honest truth about me, Rose, and about Thackeray. Now you know our secret and where we come from, and I ask that you never tell another soul, so long as you live."

Rose wiped away a tear at the corner of her eye. "I believe you."

"You do?" Thackeray asked hopefully.

Rose nodded. "You don't have to worry about me telling anyone, and if you ever need anything, just let me know."

Edmond waved a hand dismissively. "No need, but thank you. Thackeray and I have everything we will ever need right here in this forest."

Rose looked out the window and then at the time on her phone. She sighed. "I hate to leave, but I don't want my parents to worry. I'll try to come back tomorrow and the days that follow, but I can't make any promises."

Thackeray smiled and jumped from his seat. "As long as you come to visit us every now and then, it will be fine." He gave her a hug goodbye.

Rose stood up to meet Edmond and held out her hand. She wasn't on that comfortable level yet with Edmond to give him a hug, so a handshake would have to do. Edmond's story touched Rose, and she wanted to make him and Thackeray happy again.

Chapter Four

The following day Rose didn't show up, leaving Edmond and Thackeray to their daily routines: read, study music, clean the manor, cook meals, hunt, and tend to the garden. They had learned to do even the most trivial of tasks; they had to, otherwise they would not survive in this world.

Edmond decided to take it easy that day. He knew Thackeray was more than capable of doing a few more house chores on his own. The window in Edmond's room was open, letting in a nice breeze as he sat in his chair reading a book. It was one he had read many times and could probably recite word for word with his eyes closed.

The grandfather clock stood silently in the corner; it had stopped working years ago, but somehow Edmond knew when it was noon. He set down his book and rubbed his eyes. It was time for tea, his and Thackeray's favorite time of day.

Having lived three times a normal life span, Edmond and Thackeray often were at a loss for new things to talk about, but since they met Rose, a whole new world of topics had come to mind.

Edmond walked into the music room, where they usually had their tea, and Thackeray was already there, setting out the cups. He had even opened a few windows.

Thackeray turned his head and said, "Master Edmond." He took a seat and poured tea for the two of them. "How long do you think Rose will be gone?"

Edmond blew softly at his tea, making ripples. "I don't know," he said earnestly. "She never said when she would be back."

A moment of silence passed and then Thackeray said, "I wonder what the inside of Elizabeth's house looks like now."

Edmond smiled thoughtfully. "It would be interesting to see how much it's changed, wouldn't it?"

Thackeray nodded in agreement. "We should make a short visit there."

This time Edmond did not look pleased. "That would be impossible."

"How so?" asked Thackeray. "We're able to make it that far out."

"Think of the risk, Thackeray. What if someone were to see us? Besides, I don't want to be there unless Rose knows about it."

"But, master," Thackeray begged in protest.

"I said no, Thackeray!"

Thackeray set his tea cup to the side and sat back in his chair. "I'm sorry."

Edmond sighed, knowing he shouldn't have lost his temper. "I'm not saying we can never go there; I'm saying I don't feel comfortable being there without permission first."

That was not the whole truth, though. Edmond's main reason for not wanting to go was because he wasn't sure he could bear to be inside Elizabeth's old home. There were too many memories. Edmond cleared his throat. "Thackeray, will you play the piano?"

Thackeray nodded and walked over to the piano. "I'll play the usual."

As Thackeray was about to begin, Edmond asked: "Why did you ask Rose to teach you how to play? You can play wonderfully."

Thackeray looked bashful now. "When Rose first had tea with us and she was asking questions and it looked like you were in trouble, I had to do something to distract her." He grinned some and then started to play.

Thackeray played the piano so well that one would think Mozart had been his teacher or that he was Mozart himself. He struck each key gracefully and moved his hands in a perfectly fluid motion.

After they finished their tea, they returned to their chores. One they did together was cleaning the chimney. Edmond was far too big, but Thackeray was the perfect size to climb up and clean out all the soot and debris, which Edmond was in charge of disposing.

At the end of the day when their work was done, they prepared a bath for themselves in a tin tub. It was usually placed in the kitchen because it was less of a trip to haul buckets of water. Getting the bath ready took nearly an hour because they had to first heat the water over a fire. It was chilly out in the forest once the sun set, no matter the season.

When the tub was prepared, Edmond bathed first, because Thackeray was always dirtier. Having lived together for so many years, neither cared about being naked in front of the other so helping each other with back scrubs and hair washing were simple tasks.

While Edmond washed Thackeray's hair, he thought back to when he first met him. It was an incredibly cold winter night, and Edmond was heading home. He stopped at his carriage when he saw Thackeray, who was six at the time, staggering in the streets. The poor boy was practically skin and bone and wore nothing but a long shirt that barely covered his knobby knees. And his holey shoes did him no good.

Edmond remembered the weak tug on his heavy black coat as Thackeray made his way up to him. The look in Thackeray's eyes stung Edmond like a poisoned arrow. Those sunken cheeks, the empty eyes, his cold needle-like fingers, and cracked bloody lips. Death by starvation was taking over his body.

It was at that moment Edmond knew what he had to do: he scooped up Thackeray in his warm arms and lifted him into the carriage. Thackeray lay like an infant in Edmond's arms on the way back to the mansion. From then on, Thackeray always stayed at Edmond's side, and for that Edmond was grateful.

When they finished bathing, Edmond reached for his towel and grabbed Thackeray's to hand to him. It had been a long day, and they were quick to head off to bed, but not before saying good night. They slept wherever they wished. Thackeray liked sleeping in the library; he always found it comforting to be surrounded by books, plus there were blankets and pillows and sofas to curl up in.

Edmond preferred to sleep in his room. But once in a great while, he would wake up in the middle of the night and find a comfortable spot in the music room. At times he could smell Elizabeth's scent on her side of the bed, the dresses she wore, or the brush she used, and that made it unbearable to remain in his room. Tonight was different, though, as he stayed up not thinking about his beloved Elizabeth, but about Rose.

The next day Rose was still with her parents and their friends Diana and Alan. They were visiting the beach at Canvey Island. Even though Rose enjoyed the sand between her toes and the smell of the salty air, she wished she could be at the mansion. There was so much she wanted to ask Edmond and Thackeray and so much to tell them in return. But all that would have to wait.

Rose lounged in a folding chair playing with the sand as she watched the waves go in and out. Alan was grilling steaks, and the aroma made Rose salivate and her stomach growl.

Tiffany called out, "Rose, come join us!" as she laughed and danced with her husband. There was no music, but the sound of the waves and the birds was enough.

Rose wondered if she would ever find love like her parents had. But she was done sitting around and so brushed the sand off her hands and hurried to the others.

As the sun was setting over the sea, radiating a shimmering gold,

Rose wished this moment—after a day of shopping and eating amazing food at the beach—could last longer. She didn't think life could get any better.

As night fell, the four gathered their things and set out on the long drive back to the house. Rose, sitting in the back seat with a full tummy, gazed at the stars, wondering if the sky looked the same back home. Probably not, she thought, smiling to herself. It was still daytime in California. What were all of her friends doing right now? She missed them and wished she could tell them about all the amazing things she had seen so far.

That night Rose's head was filled with happy thoughts as she fell asleep.

The next morning she awoke at dawn. The room held a special kind of ambience in the emerging light. Rose smelled her hair and grimaced. It smelled like smoke and the ocean, and so did most of her body. After taking a shower, she slipped on a simple white dress with spaghetti straps. She didn't feel like doing anything with her hair that day and knew that the heat outside would dry it quickly. When Rose grabbed her handbag, she made sure her phone was inside and slipped on sandals before heading to the mansion.

Thackeray was in the front yard picking flowers when Rose arrived. A big smile spread across his face. "Good morning, Rose."

Rose smiled back and waved. "Morning, Thackeray. What are you doing?" she asked once inside the gate.

Thackeray looked down at the flower he was holding and placed it in a white cloth along with others. "Oh, I'm collecting flowers for tea." He folded up the cloth and picked up the bundle. "Won't you come inside?"

Rose nodded.

"You don't have to knock when you come over," he said, after clearing his throat. Edmond and I trust you, so just let yourself in whenever you please." He opened the two doors and stepped back to let Rose enter first. "What a nice dress, Rose. What's the occasion?" he asked with a grin.

Rose chuckled. "Just visiting you two."

Eyeing Rose's phone, Thackeray asked, "What's that in your hand? I've seen you with it before, but I felt silly asking."

Rose looked down at her phone. She had it out so she could take photos of the forest. "This is called a cellphone. A lot of people nowadays use them to communicate with people from miles away or just down the street or in another room.

"I have some things on here to show you and Edmond, if you like. Like pictures and videos."

Thackeray cocked his head to the side. "Videos?"

Rose chuckled. "I'll explain all that later." She looked around the mansion. "I haven't seen Edmond yet. Usually he's here by now."

This time Thackeray sighed. "He's still sleeping."

Rose placed her phone back in her bag and, with a mischievous smile, suggested. "We should go wake him up."

Thackeray looked shocked. "That's NOT a good idea."

"Why not?" asked Rose.

Thackeray struggled to find the right words to say. "He doesn't like to be disturbed while sleeping. I remember the first and last time I ever did that. He scolded me so badly."

Rose patted Thackeray's shoulder. "There, there. You don't have to wake him up. I will. I doubt he will yell at me. Just show me to his room, okay?"

Thackeray thought for a moment. Rose was right. Even though Edmond always got upset when someone woke him up, it was more than plausible that he wouldn't yell at Rose. In fact, he probably would prefer to be awaken by her. Thackeray nodded. "All right follow me then."

Edmond's room was far from the others, so as not to be disturbed when others began their day. But it was just he and Thackeray who lived there now.

The red satin curtains covered up most of the sun except for the little daylight that peeked through the cracks. At the end of the hall was a large door with angels at the top. Rose could see that they had once been painted, but the paint had chipped away over time.

Thackeray carefully opened the door, so as not to make a sound, and let Rose slip in. "I better stay out," he whispered and quietly closed the door.

Rose stood there silently, looking around.

Edmond's canopy bed was on the far right of the room, about twenty feet from her. A large chest sat on the floor at the foot of the bed. Dark red drapes enclosed every side. A fireplace was on the far left, the wood burned to ashes. Next to it were a chair and small corner table with a glass holding barely a mouthful of a red wine.

As Rose walked toward Edmond's bed, she admired the fox fur rug. Not wanting to get it dirty, she removed her sandals and enjoyed the feel of the fur on her bare feet.

Rose parted the drapes slowly and looked down at Edmond. She blushed when she realized he was sleeping naked. Thankfully, his silk blanket covered his most private area. She blushed but found it difficult to look away.

Carefully, Rose parted the drapes on each side of the bed and then walked over to the windows and opened those curtains. The morning sun lighted the room, and Edmond moaned, turning his head the other way. "It's time to get up, Edmond," she urged. But Edmond only stirred and continued sleeping. Finally, Rose reached over and brushed his hair away from his face. She blushed again.

Still asleep, Edmond mumbled, "Elizabeth."

Rose sighed, feeling sorry for him.

Suddenly, Edmond shot up, his head striking Rose's. He fell back onto his pillow as Rose stumbled to the floor, her hand on her head.

Edmond looked down at her. "Rose? Are you all right?" He was about to jump out of bed to see if she was okay, but quickly reconsidered, remembering he was unclothed.

"Oh, no," Rose said, moaning. "I already feel the headache." She sat up, rubbing her head.

Edmond struggled for something to say. "Rose, what are you doing in here?"

"Thackeray said it would be okay if I woke you, that you wouldn't yell at me," she replied. "He says you get upset when people wake you."

"Ah, I see." He cleared his throat. "Do you mind closing your eyes while I get dressed?"

That wasn't difficult to do being that closing her eyes lessened the pain.

Edmond quickly dressed and tied his hair back with a black string. "I'm dressed now." He walked over to Rose and held out his hand. "Do you need help getting up?"

Rose shook her head, feeling embarrassed. "No thanks. I'm okay," she said as she tried to stand up on her own. She failed and plopped her bottom back on the floor, still holding her head. "On second thought, I think I do need some help."

Edmond reached out again. "I'm really sorry about your head. I hope I didn't hurt you too much."

Rose waved a hand. "Don't worry. I'll be fine." She then remembered she wanted to show Edmond and Thackeray the pictures and videos on her phone. "Oh, I have some things to show you and Thackeray." She rubbed her head again. "Wow, you sure have a hard head."

"My apologies," Edmond said. "Shall we go meet Thackeray? I'm sure he has breakfast ready." He looked at her dress then and noticed how bare her arms and legs were. "Ah, Rose," he said, blushing. "What a lovely dress."

Rose smiled. "Thank you." She slipped her sandals back on. "Let's get going, shall we? I didn't eat anything before coming here, and breakfast sounds amazing."

"It certainly does," said Edmond.

Thackeray had cooked pancakes with homemade syrup. A bowl of grapes was there for all to share, and there was plenty of tea to go around. While they ate in the dining room, Edmond and Thackeray huddled close on either side of Rose to see what was on her phone.

"How can all of those people fit in that tiny square? Asked Thackeray: "Is that what they are? Tiny people?"

Rose giggled. "No. The phone takes a picture of whatever is in front of it. It's like painting or drawing, only this does the job instantly," Rose explained.

"Amazing," said Edmond. "Is that really you?" he asked as Rose continued to swipe through the photos and videos.

Rose nodded. "Yeah, I'm with my friends at school. It was the last day, and we were standing in the hall by our lockers." She swiped through more photos. "And these are my parents."

Thackeray smiled. "Your parents look like really nice people, Rose."

"Thanks, Thackeray. They really are. I don't know what I'd do without them. They paid for me to visit England."

Edmond suddenly asked, "You're just visiting?"

Rose nodded again. "My home is back in America. I'm only visiting

61

England till the end of the summer. I wish I could live here though."

"Then why don't you?" Thackeray asked.

Rose wasn't sure what to say. "Well, that would require a lot of time and work and, not to mention, a lot of money. Maybe someday," she told Thackeray reassuringly.

As Rose continued through her pictures and videos, Edmond started to think about his parents. He could hardly remember his father's voice. He never knew his mother, and the stories his father would tell him about her were fading.

After breakfast the trio walked to the music room.

Edmond asked, "Thackeray, will you play something for us?"

Thackeray smiled and nodded. "Of course. What would you like me to play?"

"The sonata," he replied.

Thackeray took a seat and hovered his hands over the keys. "Mozart. He is always a good choice."

Rose watched all this with a puzzled look on her face. "Wait a minute," she said. "I thought you couldn't play the piano, Thackeray?"

Thackeray paused, his face turning apple red. "I, uh, I said that to distract you when we first met. This was before you knew our secret. Edmond looked like he was in trouble, so I stepped in. Sorry to have deceived you, Rose." With that he started to play.

Rose was not surprised when she heard Thackeray playing. He was better than her, but then he had years of practice.

Edmond stood up and walked over to Rose. He bowed and held out a hand. "May I have this dance, young lady?" he asked.

Rose blushed and felt her throat get dry. She nodded shyly and took Edmond's hand.

Edmond saw her face flush and asked, "Have you ever danced

before?"

Rose shook her head slightly. "Never like this."

Edmond smiled, putting his left hand on her lower back and taking her hand with his right. "I will take you through the steps. It will be easy and fun." Edmond kept his body a respectable distance away from her as they danced. Even though no other part of his body was touching her, Rose could feel his warmth.

The moment was like something out of a children's fairytale: the princess dances with her prince for the first time. Only Rose wasn't a princess, and Edmond was not a prince, but a man literally from the past. Coming to the mansion brought Rose back in time. While dancing, she wondered if Elizabeth used to spend time with Edmond and Thackeray like this. What was she like? She must have been a good and fun-loving person. Rose couldn't see Edmond loving her otherwise.

Soon, Rose laid her head on Edmond's chest.

This surprised him, and he looked to Thackeray for help, but Thackeray only smiled, letting Edmond know that it was perfectly fine. Edmond's nerves calmed a bit, and he rested his head on top of Rose's. The dancing lessons were over for now, and the two swayed back and forth to the wonderful music.

Rose wasn't sure why she did what she did. I just want to know what it feels like, she told herself. She didn't see any harm in letting herself get a bit carried away with the moment. Her action was bold, though, and it left Edmond feeling bewildered.

Thoughts of falling in love with Edmond filled Rose's head, no matter that the idea was unrealistic. Not only was he more than two hundred years old, but he was from a completely different era and much more mature than she was. And, Rose thought, what could Edmond possibly find romantically appealing about me?

Suddenly, Rose pushed away.

Startled, Edmond asked: "What is wrong? Did you not like the dance?"

Thackeray stopped playing the piano as well.

Rose shook her head. "No, it's not that. The dance was great, thank you."

"Then what is it?" Edmond asked. He took a step toward Rose to push back some of her hair, but she moved back even farther.

"Sorry, Edmond," Rose finally said. "It's truly not your fault. I just have a lot of things on my mind right now."

Thackeray finally spoke up. "Like what, Rose? Maybe we can help you?"

Rose looked at little Thackeray. "It's honestly nothing you two need to worry about. I'm just having a dumb girly moment."

Thackeray raised a brow. "A dumb girly moment?"

Rose gave the pair a reassuring smile. She was only there for the summer and didn't need to get caught up with their lives. It wasn't fair to anyone. It was hard to tell herself this, but the harder she fought, the more she wanted to go along with it. A selfish part of her wanted Edmond all to herself.

Rose couldn't stop wondering about Elizabeth. Edmond and Thackeray were still hiding things, she knew, and they had every right to. The same went for Rose; she had hardly told them anything about herself other than where she was from and how the world worked now.

When it came down to it, Rose was just a normal girl falling for a man she hardly knew, a man who shouldn't be alive. But what if she could play with that idea for a little bit? What if she could grow closer to Edmond and Thackeray? She could always return to visit them. She could find ways to send letters, since emailing was out of the question.

"Why don't you sit down, Rose?" Edmond urged, pulling up a chair.

Rose didn't protest. Suddenly, she was very dizzy, and her stomach started to hurt.

Thackeray jumped off his seat. "I'll go get you some tea. That should help." He left so quickly that Rose didn't have time to protest.

"I really don't think this is necessary," Rose told Edmond. "What I need to do is get back to my parents. They're probably already up. I hope they haven't gone into my room yet. Maybe they think I'm still sleeping?" She was talking to herself now more than to Edmond.

Edmond put his hand on her forehead. "I think you're running a fever. Here, lie down on the sofa."

As soon as she put her head down, it started to spin even more. "A fever, you say? Oh, great."

Edmond lifted her head to prop a small pillow underneath. "I hope that helps," he said.

Rose could only nod.

"I'm sure Thackeray will bring a wet cloth with him as well," Edmond said.

Rose could hardly respond. "Right." And she passed out.

Rose lay half awake. Her headache was gone, and her fever had gone down. Even with her eyes closed, she could see light flickering. She moaned a little and heard Edmond speak to her softy.

"Rose? How are you feeling?"

Rose slowly opened her eyes to see Edmond standing over her. She looked around as best as she could and noticed she was lying in his bed. "What time is it?" she asked.

"It's nearly dark," he said.

Rose gasped. "Oh, shit!" She sat up, trying to get off the bed, but

Edmond, a little taken aback by her choice of words, forced her to lie back down. "Excuse me, Rose, but you still have a small fever."

Rose pushed Edmond's hands away and sat back up. "I have to get back to the house, Edmond. My parents have probably already called the police. I need to go back now!" Tears formed in her eyes. She was more than serious.

Edmond brushed away a stray tear that found its way down her cheek. "No need to worry, little one. Thackeray has already taken care of that."

Rose took a few breaths before asking, "What are you talking about?"

Edmond smiled. "Thackeray made up a sleeping powder as soon as we realized you could not be moved a great distance. He went to the house and slipped it inside whilst your parents were preoccupied. The power travels a great distance from where it is placed. And no need to worry; the powder is harmless. It helped your parents fall asleep."

"Are you sure it won't hurt them?" Rose asked. "And how long will they be asleep?"

Edmond nodded. "Thackeray stayed to make sure nothing bad happened. Your parents should be asleep for about twelve hours, maybe more." He grabbed a wet cloth from a bowl, wrung the water from it, and dabbed Rose's cheeks.

Rose sighed, feeling more relaxed. "Thank you." She stared at the fireplace, the light from it making her eyes look a blazing blue.

From time to time Edmond would stroke Rose's arms and hands with the wet cloth and even massage her hands, trying his best to make sure she was as comfortable as possible. All the while, he hummed a little tune.

Rose looked over at Edmond and asked, "Edmond? What's that song you're humming?"

Edmond continued to massage her hands. "Just a song I heard a long time ago."

"I don't believe you," Rose scoffed.

Edmond finally looked up. "And why do you think that?"

Rose said nothing for a second, instead studying his face. "I can see it in your eyes."

Edmond said nothing.

Rose repositioned herself on the bed. "What was she like? I want to know more about her."

"About whom?" he asked.

Rose rolled her eyes. "Don't play dumb, Edmond."

At last Edmond said, "Elizabeth," her name rolling off his tongue like a pebble sinking to the bottom of a pond.

Rose nodded, hoping she was getting somewhere with this conversation. "It's not good to keep things bottled up inside," she told him. "Sometimes it can help to talk about it."

There was a long pause before Edmond said, "Because it hurts." Another pause. "But you're right; I should talk about it. I've never even told Thackeray exactly what happened to Elizabeth. It would break his heart even more if he knew."

Rose said, "So you will tell me?"

"I will," he said. "And, in fact, you remind me of her. In small ways, but still you do."

Rose was moved to hear this. "I do?"

Edmond nodded. "Yes. In fact, she was about as old as you when we married."

Curious, Rose asked, "How old was she?"

Edmond smiled a bit, remembering the good days. "She was

seventeen."

Rose's eyes grew wide. "Only seventeen," she said in disbelief, knowing she shouldn't have been shocked at all to hear this. "And how old are you now, Edmond?"

"Honestly," Edmond started, "it's been ages since I've celebrated a birthday, but if you really must know, I'm two-hundred-fifty-four."

Rose gasped. "But you're forever twenty-two, huh?" Again, she knew she shouldn't have been surprised, but she was. "You're old, Edmond." She almost laughed.

A grin appeared on his face. "Ah, I see you're feeling better. That's good." He cleared his throat. "Do you still want me to tell you?"

Rose nodded eagerly.

Edmond put the cloth back in the bowl and took in a deep breath, preparing himself. "It happened in eighteen-eighty on a cold fall morning. I had spent my last night with her."

Rose could see him struggling and wondered if she should tell him to stop.

Edmond continued on. "I can still recall the smell of her hair and feel of her skin as she often curled up next to me. But when I awoke that morning, I was alone and the fireplace was cool."

As Edmond's words poured out, Rose imagined everything taking place.

Edmond had heard the neigh of a horse, and he sprung from his bed in haste to look out the window. Elizabeth could be seen in her nightgown leaving on the horse. Befuddled and alarmed, Edmond ran from his room, not bothering to put on shoes, only wearing his breeches.

Thackeray was still asleep, so there was no need to waken or worry him.

Edmond set out on foot to find Elizabeth. She had taken the only horse, so he was forced to run after her, taking as many shortcuts as possible to try to reach her. He called out to her many times, but she did not stop. Did she not hear him?

By this time Edmond had learned his boundaries on how far out he could go, and Elizabeth was pushing that limit. It pained him to think of what she might do.

Edmond tripped, spraining his ankle. He picked himself up, ignoring the pain, and unrelentingly continued his quest to catch Elizabeth. He could feel himself getting weaker—not because he was running out of breath, but because his body was changing. He was challenging the distance he could go. His body was shrinking to nothing but frail bones and wrinkly skin, his hair turning gray. He wasn't sure what would happen to him if he ventured any farther, but Elizabeth was still out there, and he knew he had to go on.

At last he saw Elizabeth get off the horse and set out on foot. She was headed toward the river. Edmond called out to her again as he watched her run to a dock. She was fumbling around with a boat that was tied up, and when she heard Edmond call out her name again, she looked up for a second, only to hasten with the knot. Her beautiful blond hair had turned white and her skin wrinkled with age. But there was something else: her face was sullied with tears.

"Come back, Elizabeth! What are you doing?" Edmond was nearly there.

Elizabeth jumped into the boat and pushed away from the dock just before Edmond could reach her. She was only a few feet away now, but the distance was widening as Edmond found himself paralyzed by fear. He wanted to jump into the water and bring Elizabeth back, but he couldn't move and just stared helplessly at her.

Suddenly, Elizabeth smiled as she reached out. "Come with me," she said.

Edmond pleaded with her. "Elizabeth, please come back." He couldn't reach her hand. And then, right before his eyes, Elizabeth stood rigid for a second, her smile lingering. Her body turned to ash, and all that remained in the boat were a pile of her ashes and clothes.

Edmond lost his breath and fell to his knees. His whole body shook as he screamed. He sobbed and heaved, trying in vain to control his emotions. Even after the boat had disappeared down the river, Edmond sat there in dismay.

"I cried her name over and over, hoping she would come back and everything would be just as it was."

Edmond was coming at an end with his story. "You ask me, Rose, what Elizabeth was like. She was many things. It's so hard to put it into words. You wanted to know what happened. Now you may be wondering why Thackeray and I have chosen to stay here."

Rose nodded.

"We cannot give up on life no matter what the circumstances are. As long as Thackeray and I are still breathing, we will continue on with our lives. You're here with us now. That proves that our time waiting here has not been all for naught. Elizabeth chose to leave. It was her choice, not mine or Thackeray's. This is our home; this is our life." He stopped, unable to say anymore.

Rose reached out and grabbed Edmond's hand. She knew that he still loved Elizabeth. She was right, though; Edmond no longer had to keep that terrible secret to himself.

Chapter Five

Early the next morning the sun shined in through the cracks of the curtains. Birds could be heard chirping and other animals running around outside. As Rose was waking up, she rubbed her face against the pillow and yawned. She brought the blanket up to her face and snuggled with it. When she remembered where she was, she shot up. That's right, she thought, I stayed the night at the mansion.

The thought of her parents came to mind, and she soon remembered the powder Thackeray left behind there. She knew she didn't have much time though. She grabbed her sandals and bag and tried to tiptoe out of the room.

But the door creaked as she opened it, and Edmond, still asleep, stirred in his chair. Rose looked back, hoping he wouldn't wake, but he did. He yawned and looked over at Rose with tired eyes.

"Are you leaving?" Edmond asked.

Rose nodded as she stood by the door. "I have to. I'm worried about my parents still."

Edmond stood up from his chair and stretched his arms. "I trust you're feeling better then?"

"I am. Thank you."

Edmond grabbed a red coat that was hanging on the side of the chair and placed it over Rose's shoulders. She seemed to have disappeared in it, but her head poked out from underneath. "Take this with you in case it rains."

Rose repositioned the coat so that it fit better. "Thanks again, Edmond. I'll come back to see you and Thackeray. I just don't know when."

Edmond smiled. "You're welcome. You best be off then," he said with a quick bow.

As Rose made her way back to the house, she suddenly stopped. She thought she had seen someone in the woods. At first she thought that maybe someone was out taking a walk, for there were trails all over the woods. But if anyone was out there, surely she would have gotten a good look at them. For a second Rose thought she saw the figure or a shadow of a female. She didn't want to stand around much longer and began to run.

When she reached the house, she found her mother passed out on the couch and the television on.

Her father seemed to have just awaken and sat at the kitchen table with a cup of coffee and a newspaper. "You're up early," he said. "Where did you get that coat?"

Rose opened the fridge and pulled out a drink. "From the attic."

Her father nodded and took a sip of his coffee. "It looks too warm to wear in weather like this."

Rose shrugged. "It might rain."

Rose headed up to her room and plopped on the bed. She wrapped Edmond's coat tighter around her. The scent of him and the mansion were all over the coat. She lay back on her bed, thinking about the events that took place the day before. Perhaps all the excitement was what made her feel ill. She then thought of Elizabeth and what Edmond had said. How could Elizabeth just leave without saying goodbye? There must have been a good reason.

Rose was awakened from her dreamy trance by a knock on her door. She sat up quickly and took the coat off.

It was Lucas. "Are you hungry?" he asked. "Your mom just woke up, and I was thinking of making breakfast."

The mention of food made Rose's stomach growl. She hadn't eaten for twenty-four hours. "I'm starved," she told him.

Lucas smiled. "Great. I'm going to make tons of pancakes."

Great, thought Rose. More pancakes. "Sounds nice, Dad."

Lucas was about to leave but turned back around: "Your mom and I were talking about going fishing. We thought we could do that later today and maybe have another cookout. Do you want to come?"

"Are we going to the beach again?" Rose asked hopefully.

Lucas shook his head. "No, some place closer. Alan told me there is a nice river in the forest with plenty of fish."

Rose remembered Edmond telling her about the river, and she wondered if it was the same one. Then again, the forest was huge, and it could be in a totally different direction. If her parents happened to come anywhere near the mansion, she would distract them and lead them in the opposite direction. "Yeah, I'll come." She got up from her bed. "Let me put on more comfortable clothes, and I'll meet you down in the kitchen to help with breakfast."

Rose had never gone fishing with her parents before. She would have preferred to stay indoors and watch television, but circumstances were different. California was far away and aside from Thackeray and Edmond, she had no one else but her parents and their friends to hang out with.

If her parents found the mansion, they would definitely tell Alan and Diana, and soon others would know. Word would get out, and Edmond and Thackeray would be forced to leave. Rose couldn't let that happen, so she had to go fishing.

After breakfast Rose helped her parents load the car with fishing gear. They would be driving to a different opening to the forest. Perhaps it would lead them farther from the mansion.

When they arrived at the river, Lucas pulled out a hat like his from a large bag and handed it to Rose. "To become a real fisherman, you have to wear this cap."

Rose pushed her father's hand away. "No, thanks."

Lucas looked disappointed. "What? Is it not your style? Try it on. You might like it." He plopped it on his daughter's head, despite what she said, and continued.

There was a rustic store and dock on the way, and Rose's parents stopped to purchase a boat.

Tiffany looked up while loading the fishing gear in the boat and said: "Get in, Rose. The boat is safe."

That wasn't what Rose was worried about. "I'm not scared of the boat," she said. "I'm just no good at fishing."

Lucas laughed. "You've never tried fishing, so how would you know?"

"I just know," Rose said as she climbed into the boat.

The boat drifted slowly for more than an hour, and Rose still had no fish to claim. Her parents had netted more than enough fish for that night's supper and were still catching more. All that Rose could get were minnows and countless ripples of fish that were taunting her. She pulled her net out of the water and sighed. Maybe it was her side of the boat, and her parents were stealing all the fish before she could catch any. Rose decided to try another solution and grabbed the fishing rod.

The tackle box was full of bait, and Rose reached in for a worm. As she struggled to get it on the hook, the boat continued to float on.

Once she had hooked her worm, Rose looked up to cast out her line when she suddenly stopped. The river was coming to a split. She looked up at the trees to see if anything looked familiar, but none did.

Soon, though, Rose spotted a moss-covered dock far down the river. It was broken, and half of it lay in the water.

"I think we should go the other way," Rose said, breaking her silence.

Tiffany turned her head. "No talking. You'll scare the fish," she whispered.

Rose pressed on. "I'm serious, you guys. I think I saw a weird animal."

Lucas' head jerked up. "Where?"

Tiffany sighed and pulled her bait out of the water. "I guess we have plenty of fish. Let's turn back and find a nice place to have lunch."

Rose was more than happy to be done with fishing and badly wanted to get out of the cramped boat. "Yes, please. And make sure it's far from here."

"Did you really see an animal?" Lucas asked.

Rose nodded. "It was big and hairy. Now let's go."

Tiffany and Lucas put their nets away, grabbed their oars and started heading in the opposite direction.

They found a nice spot with plenty of soft grass to lay down a blanket and eat their lunch. They had packed ham and cheese sandwiches, potato chips, fruit, juice, and water.

When Rose had her fill of food, she stood up to brush the crumbs off her lap. "I need to take a walk and stretch my legs after being in that boat all morning."

Tiffany looked up at her daughter. "Didn't you say you saw a big hairy animal? Maybe you should just wait for us to finish eating."

Rose sighed. "I saw the animal on the other side of the forest. I'll be fine, okay? I promise I won't go far."

Lucas shook his head. "No, Rose. I think you should stay."

Rose protested. "I'll just be right over there." She pointed to her right. "If anything happens, I'll yell for help. Besides, I haven't explored the forest yet." She lied, for her main reason was to check out the dock they had passed earlier. She left before her parents could say more. "I'll just be a minute, I swear. I just want to take some pictures." She wasn't lying about that.

This side of the forest was different from what she was used to seeing. It had multiple trails leading in all directions, with signs posted to assist hikers.

Rose walked along the riverbank to make it easier to find her way back. She was gone more than a minute, she knew, and would have to turn back soon so her parents wouldn't worry.

Eventually, she came across the dock, which was on the opposite side of the river. Good, she thought. I just have to keep my parents away from that side. The river seemed so still. Not like earlier, when she was in the boat with her parents. The dock looked desolate. Rose looked down the river, knowing the events that had transpired there long ago, and felt a shiver down her spine.

She continued down the river to where it curved. There was a compound of openings on this side, leading the water in every direction, but on one side the river came to an end and finally met up with land. Rose walked closer to it, but suddenly stopped. Lying a few feet from her, hidden in moss and grass and broken tree limbs, was the half-submerged remains of a small boat. Most of it had rotted away.

Curious, Rose walked up to the boat and reached inside. The moss was slick and smelled sour. This can't be the same boat, can it? she thought. It just can't be. Something shiny caught her attention, and she cleared some of the debris. It was a silver necklace with a heart-shaped gold locket. Rose tried to open it, but the latch wouldn't budge.

She looked up from the necklace when she felt droplets of rain on her head. She hurried back to her parents, who were already packing up the

76

boat.

"Did you see any hairy animals?" Lucas asked.

Rose shook her head. "No." She slipped the necklace into the pocket of her jeans and got in the boat.

"You were right about the rain," said Lucas.

That night Rose sat in the upstairs bathroom cleaning the necklace, all the while smelling the fish her father was cooking downstairs. When she finished getting the dirt off the necklace, Rose wiped it dry with a hand towel. Examining it further, she noticed a name engraved ever so finely on the back of the locket: Elizabeth Ann Gray.

Rose held her breath for a moment, and when she looked up at the mirror, she saw a woman standing behind her for a split second. Rose gasped and nearly dropped the necklace down the drain.

A knock at the door made Rose flinch.

"Rose? Are you in there?" It was her mother.

Rose calmed herself. "Yeah, I'm just washing up before we eat."

"Oh, okay. Well, come down in two minutes. Your dad is just about done cooking the fish."

"Okay." Rose didn't move until she couldn't hear her mother's footsteps any longer. She reached for the door knob, then froze, clenching the necklace in her fist as her heart began to race. Rose was not alone in the room, or so it seemed. She turned her head and pressed her back against the door.

A young, blond female stood about six feet away. Her hair was long and messy, and she wore a simple, light-blue satin V-neck dress with long sleeves. The dress was tattered, but her pale skin was pristine. The look on her face was relaxed.

"Go away," Rose whispered. "Please, go away." She closed her eyes and repeated herself. When she opened them again, the woman was gone.

Rose hurried out of the bathroom, her legs shaking. She gathered her thoughts and steadied her breaths before joining her parents for dinner. And as she looked down at the name on the necklace, she thought, maybe Diana is right to believe in ghosts.

Chapter Six

Rose's birthday arrived, and she spent the day visiting Dover castle with her parents and Alan and Diana. Rose had never seen anything so magnificent in all her life. To have walked where so many others had before her was mind-boggling. She was literally standing on history.

Her cheeks flushed with excitement. She had already taken nearly a hundred pictures with her father's Canon camera, and more were to come.

Diana approached Rose as she crouched to take a photo. "Are you enjoying yourself?"

Rose snapped a picture and stood back up. "I am. I love it here."

Diana smiled. "Good. I wouldn't want you being bored on your birthday. How old are you now?"

"Nineteen," Rose answered.

Diana was about to walk off and meet up with Alan, but Rose stopped her. "What is it, dear?"

Rose had acted without thinking and struggled to come up with something to say. "Do you really believe in ghosts?"

Diana smiled, happy that Rose brought up such a topic. "Of course, I do. Why do you ask? Have you seen one?" she asked.

Rose's face turned a more intense pink. "Oh, no, I haven't. I was just wondering."

"That's too bad," said Diana.

Their conversation was short-lived as Alan called out to them to catch up.

After exploring the castle Rose visited the gift shop. She hadn't yet bought anything for her friends and family back home, so this was a great opportunity to bring them a little something from England.

The five went to a beach later that day and then visited the White Cliffs. They were breathtaking. Rose had spent a month in England by now and would have to say goodbye to it and all its glory in just two more months.

Oftentimes, she would think she was dreaming because she felt so lucky. She thought about what Thackeray had said about her coming back to England and visiting them. At least she would have a free place to stay, if she came back.

That night, as Rose was getting ready for bed, she took the necklace out of her pocket and set it on the nightstand. She had carried it with her all day, too afraid to leave it alone. She didn't want to wear it either, thinking that would be an insult to Elizabeth. I have to take the necklace back to Edmond tomorrow, she thought. He deserved to have it.

Something in the middle of the night woke Rose. She tried her best to block out the sound, but the longer she tried to ignore it, the louder it became. At first she thought it was just the sound of the wind, but nothing was rattling the window. The sound was coming from within her room.

The moaning slowly turned into sobs. Rose pulled her blanket over her head, her heart thumping, and she hoped that whatever was making that sound would go away. But it didn't. Whatever it was was moving around the room now. Rose could hear it near the end of the bed. It grabbed the blanket and yanked it.

No matter how tightly Rose held on, her blanket would slip off, and she would feel the rush of air. Rose tried to see whatever it was that was standing at the foot of her bed. In a flash the female figure now straddled her.

She was trapped.

A pair of icy blue eyes looked down at her, and Rose realized that the female was the same one she had seen in the bathroom. She wore the same dress, and her hair was still a mess. As she reached toward Rose's face, she gently caressed her cheek.

"Elizabeth?" Rose finally managed to say.

The female bolted upright, and a baby's cry rang in Rose's ears. The female paused for a moment and then, walking backward off the bed, disappeared into the shadows.

Rose bolted upright and turned on the lamp. She looked at the clock and groaned. It was only four in the morning, but it would be impossible for her to sleep now. Still, she was afraid to get out of bed, and it was some time before she felt safe to leave her room. She opened the door to her parents' bedroom a crack, but they were asleep, so she left.

She tried watching television, flipping through pictures and videos on her phone, and even reading, but nothing could get her mind off the girl she saw and the sounds of a baby crying. It wasn't just her imagination. Rose had seen her twice now as clearly as she could see her own hands. What she needed was someone to talk to, and her parents were definitely out of the question.

By now it was five in the morning. Rose slipped on shoes and headed outside.

Fog was blocking the rising sun, so everything was obscured in shades of gray. Rose could see only a few feet ahead of her, so she decided to use the flashlight on her phone.

The birds were singing, the owls were asleep, and the insects were nowhere to be seen or heard. The only sounds echoing in the forest were Rose's footsteps crushing leaves or snapping twigs.

Rose spotted a faint light ahead. It had to be from the mansion. But something else was glowing in the distance: a pair of yellow eyes. In time the fog lifted to reveal the gray silhouette of a wolf.

Rose picked up her speed, trying to gain distance between her and

81

the wolf. When that failed, she picked up a rock and threw it in its direction. For a moment the wolf was stunned and stopped chasing Rose, but her actions only angered it.

Frightened, Rose tripped and fell flat on her tummy. She tried to scramble to her feet but kept slipping, and she thought her end was near, with the wolf ready to pounce. But just then a cloaked figure approached from the side of the trail and, with a swift swing of its ax, slashed the gut of the wolf, sending it flying backward. The cloaked figure then ran to the wolf and finished the job with a chop to its head.

When it was over, Rose sat there trembling as the cloaked figure stood by, still holding the bloody ax. As it turned to face Rose, it lifted its hood, and there stood Edmond. "Rose? Are you all right?"

Rose nodded, unable to speak.

Edmond cleaned the wolf's blood off the ax with his cloak. "What are you doing out here at this hour?" he asked, lending her a hand.

"I needed to see you," she said.

"Whatever for?" he asked. "Is everything all right at the house?"

Rose nodded. "Yes, of course." She then thought of the ghostly figure. "Well, sort of. That's why I need to talk to you. I think you could help me. Plus, I need to show you something very important."

Before Edmond could respond, Thackeray came rushing out of the bushes with a large white sack. "I see you finally got him." He walked over to the wolf and started shoving the carcass into the bag. He looked over at Edmond and then at Rose. "Rose? What are you doing here?" he asked, surprised to see her.

"I came here to talk to Edmond." She looked at Edmond, but he had since turned his gaze back to the wolf.

"Thackeray, take the wolf back to the mansion quick as you can. I'll take Rose back to the house."

Rose scoffed. "Excuse me, but I need to talk to you about something seriously important."

"It can wait," Edmond said.

Rose backed away quickly, refusing to leave. "I'm not going until you listen to me."

Edmond glanced over at Thackeray. "Go, Thackeray!" he ordered.

When Thackeray was well out of sight, Edmond turned to Rose, "What do you need to tell me?"

Rose huffed. "I can see you're used to getting your way, but it won't be that way with me, especially if it's something important." She paused. "But can we please talk about it at the mansion. I'm getting a very uneasy feeling standing out here."

Edmond sighed, giving in to Rose. "All right, I'll take you back to the mansion." He noticed that she was favoring her right side. "Did you hurt yourself?" he asked.

Rose looked down at her left ankle, which was beginning to swell. "I hurt my ankle when I fell. I can't really stand on it."

"Oh, then allow me." Edmond bent down and picked up Rose bridal style. "Is this better?"

Rose blushed. "Uh, yeah. Thank you." She didn't think it would be so easy to change his mind.

"You're right about what you said," Edmond began. "I am used to getting my way, and that makes me a hard person to live with sometimes. Just ask Thackeray." He almost laughed. "But you, Rose, you're different. You're headstrong, and you speak your mind. I like that."

Rose smiled a little. "That's because I'm from a different time," she said softly.

When they reached the mansion, a fire was already going in the great hall. Edmond set Rose down on a sofa and took a seat.

For a moment there was nothing but the sound of the crackling fire to interrupt the silence in the room.

"You and Thackeray seemed well prepared for that wolf," Rose started.

Edmond relaxed in the chair. "We've had our eyes set on that wolf for a few weeks now. It had been killing the animals we hunt here. We were worried that it would kill everything off within the area."

"I guess I was very lucky then," Rose said. "Thank you for that, by the way."

"You're very welcome," Edmond said, clearing his throat. "Now what was it that you needed to tell me?"

Rose took a breath and looked at the fire. "I had a nightmare…at least I think it was a nightmare."

Edmond remained silent.

"I think," said Rose, "that the girl I saw was Elizabeth." She looked over at Edmond, who stared back at her.

"Why do you think that?" Edmond asked.

Rose opened her mouth to say something but stopped.

Edmond leaned forward. "Rose, you can tell me," he reassured her.

"I've seen paintings of her at the house. I'm sure it's Elizabeth." She opened her hand and showed him the necklace. "I also found this."

Edmond stood up and took the necklace, examining it closely. "Where did you find this?"

Rose also stood up, forgetting for a moment about her painful ankle. "Is it Elizabeth's? It is, right?"

The two stood there silently as Edmond looked nostalgically at the necklace. "It is Elizabeth's. Where did you come by this?"

"My parents and I went fishing the other day. We passed by a dock, and at first I wondered if it was the same dock you described in your story.

When we stopped for lunch, I walked ahead of my parents and found a boat almost rotted away. Lying inside was this necklace."

Edmond turned to Rose and smiled. "Thank you so much for returning this to me. It truly means the world to me."

"Of course," she said. "It wasn't mine to keep in the first place. I knew I had to give it to you."

Edmond put the necklace in his pocket. "Was there something else you needed to tell me?"

Rose thought for a moment and nodded. "Yes, there is."

Edmond waited patiently.

"When I saw Elizabeth standing in front of me, she had this look about her as if she was tired or something."

Edmond sighed and sat back in the chair, sinking into it. "Elizabeth wasn't always the way you just described her. But in time she grew to be a very unsettling person." He paused. "I'm partly to blame."

"Do you want to talk about it?"

Edmond seemed almost lost in thought. Just when Rose thought he was going to shut himself down, he said: "Elizabeth was the only child. Before she was born, her mother had lost four children in infancy and more with miscarriages, so when she was born, she was always watched over. It wasn't until her fourteenth birthday that her parents loosened their grip on her."

"I don't blame them," said Rose. "Elizabeth was their miracle baby. Of course, they were overly protective. I would be, too."

"Indeed," Edmond said, nodding in agreement. "Tell me more about your nightmare."

Rose sat back on the sofa before saying: "Before Elizabeth disappeared, I heard a baby cry. It was so sad."

Edmond crossed his arms and looked off to the side, thinking: "That sounds very disturbing. I hope it doesn't happen again."

Rose narrowed her eyes. "What's wrong, Edmond?"

Edmond shrugged. "Nothing."

"You're lying to me." Rose confronted him. "Edmond?"

Still he said nothing.

Rose almost got out of her seat but thought better of it, for the sake of her ankle. "What happened to me means something, doesn't it?"

Edmond glanced over at her and again looked away.

At that moment Rose had an idea of what was on Edmond's mind. "Elizabeth had a baby, didn't she?"

Edmond finally stood up and walked over to the fireplace, jabbing a charred log with a poker. "You seem to have forgotten your place, Miss Rose Fair. What you say is too bold."

Rose stood up abruptly, almost falling because of the pain in her ankle, but she stood her ground. "Forgive me if I am sticking my nose into your business, but when Elizabeth's ghost comes to visit me, it becomes my business."

"There is still so much you don't know, Rose," Edmond said.

Rose placed a hand on his shoulder. "Then help me understand. Tell me everything. Let me help you, Edmond."

"You can't help me," he said, pushing her hand away. "It has already been done."

Rose took a step back. "At first, I wasn't sure I wanted to be here," she started. "I hadn't been here in England for a full day, and already I wanted to retreat to my old room. But now I think I understand why I've come here, and it's not because of a graduation present."

Edmond said, "And what reason is that?"

"To help you and Thackeray, and I can't do that unless you open up to me completely." She looked at him sternly.

Edmond grasped Rose's hands and squeezed them gently. "You are too sweet, Rose. But I don't think I can ever be saved, no matter what I tell you." He rested his forehead on top of hers. "Yet here you are, trying your best. It's so sweet of you, honestly."

Rose whispered. "Why do you think you can't be saved? You're such a kind person."

Edmond gave her a tense smile. "You think I'm kind?"

Rose nodded.

"Tell me, Rose," he said. "What kind of person do you think I am?"

Rose had known Edmond for only a few weeks and thought carefully before answering. "You're a kind person who has been hurt repeatedly. You have learned from that pain, making your will strong. That's why you're still here. There are still things for you to do, people to help. You haven't let the past claim your high spirits. If that were the case, I wouldn't be here. In short, you're a kind and strong-willed person, Edmond." She took a step back and looked up at him, adding: "I know there is a lot more for you to tell me. The same goes for Thackeray. I need you to put your full trust in me and tell me everything." Rose had said all she could to help Edmond open up to her. She released his hands and sat down again.

Edmond remained standing. "I think the year was eighteen-seventy," he began. "The three of us had lived in solitude for a long time. We had memorized each other's footsteps walking through the mansion. We no longer cared what time of day we had our tea or took our naps. It seemed like nothing was ever going to change. The forest stayed the same; we stayed the same. But something inside Elizabeth did change. She was longing for more.

"It turned out that Elizabeth wanted a family. When she told me this, I was happy, but I didn't know if it was possible since the potion had many effects."

Rose spoke up. "Did you tell her that?"

"Of course I did. But she didn't care; she wanted to try, and so we did. The outcome was not a satisfying one. Elizabeth kept having miscarriages. I didn't know how to help her. I feared she shared the same fate as her mother." Edmond cleared his throat, and when he started to speak again, the scene became vivid in Rose's mind.

Early one summer morning Elizabeth awoke to a throbbing pain in her gut and slipped off the bed. She grabbed a bucket that was sitting underneath and vomited.

Edmond woke up to the sound of her purging and ran to her side. "Are you all right, Elizabeth? Tell me what's wrong." He went to cradle her in his arms, but she was freezing to the touch. "My God, Elizabeth, you're freezing!"

When Elizabeth finished puking, Edmond held her in his arms. At first, she started to laugh and then she began to cry, her whole body shaking.

Edmond was confused and didn't know what to do for her. "Tell me what's wrong, Elizabeth. Tell me so I can help take away the pain."

Elizabeth quieted her sobs and dabbed at her tears. "Nothing is wrong, Edmond. I'm happy."

"Happy?" said Edmond.

Elizabeth slowly nodded her head. "I'm with child."

Edmond was flabbergasted. "Are you certain?"

Elizabeth stopped shaking, and her body warmed. "Yes, I'm certain."

Lying there together, they both started to tear up, happy to have another opportunity to have a family of their own.

As the months went by, Edmond and Thackeray made sure Elizabeth had plenty of food and rest. She bathed nearly every night, and Thackeray put on sock puppet plays for her when she was bedridden.

When the day came for Elizabeth to give birth, she was taking a walk with Thackeray in the back yard. She stopped in mid-sentence and grasped his shoulder as water began trickling down her legs.

"Is it time?" he asked, steadying her.

Elizabeth nodded frantically. "Go get Edmond. I can't walk." She let go of Thackeray and leaned against a brick wall.

Thackeray ran with all his might, never stopping until he found Edmond. He was out in the woods hunting when Thackeray told him the news. Together they rushed back to the mansion.

Edmond picked up Elizabeth effortlessly, his adrenaline kicking in. He took to their bedchamber and gathered all of the sheets.

Thackeray brought over a bowl of boiling water and one that was cool.

There was no doctor to help them, so they were on their own. They did everything they could for Elizabeth, but it seemed all their time preparing for the birth was not enough. One thing was for certain: Elizabeth would not die. She couldn't. No matter how much blood she lost, she would only faint from time to time.

After twelve hours of labor, Elizabeth finally had her baby.

With bloody, shaking arms, Edmond handed Elizabeth their baby boy. She looked down at her son and smiled. He was so small and innocent, yet so full of life. But abruptly, Elizabeth stopped smiling and ordered Edmond and Thackeray out of the room.

She was alone with the baby.

Elizabeth looked at her son's frail body—his fingers, toes, and even his little nose. In a small way Elizabeth was jealous of her own son. He was more human than she; at least that's how she felt as she began to cry.

His life is not a lie like mine, she thought to herself. "I don't deserve you," she whispered softly.

As the days passed, Elizabeth seemed to be at her happiest. Benjamin, as they called him, brought the household enormous joy, and Elizabeth found a reason to keep going.

Little Benji was growing up healthy. When Edmond and Elizabeth were not around, Thackeray was his playmate.

But one day, as Elizabeth was putting him down for his nap, she sang him to sleep and caressed his skin as he closed his eyes. She did this almost every time, and when it came time for him to wake up, little Benji lay there still. Elizabeth shook him gently, trying to wake him, and whispered in his ear.

Elizabeth finally came to the terrible realization that her son was dead. He was only two months old.

The timing couldn't have been any worse. Edmond had just walked into the room. When Elizabeth turned to face him with tears gushing from her eyes, Edmond's heart sank. "No," he said. He didn't want to accept his son's fate.

Elizabeth forced herself to spit out, "He's dead."

Unlike Elizabeth, Edmond showed his grief in a different way. He grabbed a vase from atop the fireplace and threw it against the wall.

Elizabeth jumped at the sound. "Stop, Edmond. Wrecking our room is not going to bring our son back!"

Edmond shot back at her. "Why," he spat out. "Why should I stop? After everything we have done to keep our son alive!" It was then that he started to cry. "Where's the potion? Let's try that," he mumbled, pacing back and forth.

"The potion won't work on someone who is dead, Edmond," Elizabeth told him as she walked up to him. She put arm around him, and they cried together.

A tiny knock sounded on the door, and Thackeray poked his head in. "I thought I heard something break. Is everything okay?" He looked past them and toward the crib where the dead infant lay. "What's wrong?" he asked them.

Elizabeth sniffed, dabbing at her tears. "Oh, Thackeray…" her voice trailing off.

Thackeray bit down on his lip to stop it from quivering, but he could not and ran out of the room. He was not one to let others see him cry.

Edmond turned to Elizabeth and kissed her forehead. "We need to get a burial ready for Benjamin right away."

Horrified at the mention of burying their son, Elizabeth stepped over to Benji and picked up his body. "This is my baby," she said, holding him close to her heart. "He doesn't deserve to be put in the cold ground."

Edmond wiped away his tears. "Don't do this, Elizabeth." He reached for the infant.

Elizabeth turned to the side. "I can't," she told him. "I just can't."

Edmond sighed, still fighting to control his tears. "Benjamin is gone, Elizabeth. We have to give him a proper grave. We can't just let him lie here. It's not right."

Grave? Elizabeth didn't want to think about it. Finally, she said, "Please, give me a moment."

Edmond nodded. "As you wish," he said and gave her a small bow before leaving the room.

Elizabeth laid her son on the bed and dressed him in an outfit she had sewn just a few weeks earlier. She then wrapped him in his blanket.

It looked as if Benjamin was only sleeping.

Elizabeth's heart shattered. "I never wanted this," she said to herself.

At last she picked up her son and carried him to the great room, where Edmond and Thackeray were waiting.

Thackeray's eyes were red and puffy, and Edmond kept his gaze from the infant.

"Let's go," he said, gripping a shovel in his hands.

The trio walked to the back of the property where those who had died in the massacre were buried.

The muffled sound of the shovel blade striking the ground made their skin crawl.

Elizabeth looked at her son as if he would wake up from his nap soon, but he never did. He never would. And when it came time to place his body in the grave, Elizabeth peered down into it. She couldn't help but think that this was where her baby would stay from now on.

Edmond reached for the baby, but Elizabeth wouldn't budge. "Elizabeth," he spoke softly. "Give me Benjamin, please." He sighed. "Do you want to do it?" he asked.

Elizabeth said nothing and pushed her way past Edmond. She was careful about getting into the grave, and as she took her first step, tears again welled up in her eyes. As she placed him on the cold ground, she kissed his cheeks before covering his face with the the blanket.

Edmond helped Elizabeth out of the grave and started to throw dirt back into the hole.

Both Thackeray and Elizabeth looked a way as the dirt piled onto Benjamin's little body. They wanted to walk away, having had enough, but they knew it best to stay.

After what seemed like a long wait, Edmond patted the dirt gently with the shovel and then tossed it to the side, glad to get rid of it. As the three walked back to the mansion, Elizabeth grabbed Edmond's hand. Thackeray went on ahead, knowing she wanted to speak to Edmond in private.

She cupped his face with her hands and said: "No matter what happens, I'll forgive you. And no matter what we say to each other, I will always love you." Elizabeth kissed him, leaving him stunned and walked on ahead.

Edmond sat alone on the back steps of the mansion for a while. He could hear the faint sound of Elizabeth playing the piano, and finally he wept for his son.

Rose waited for Edmond to say something else. "What happened after that?" she asked.

Edmond took in a deep breath and said: "We tried for another child, and the birth was easier this time." Edmond smiled faintly at the memory. "We had a beautiful baby girl. She looked so much like Elizabeth."

Rose smiled at this.

"But," said Edmond, "I don't know what happened to her."

Rose raised a brow. "What do you mean?"

Edmond scanned the room, as if that would help him find an answer. "I don't know."

Rose was confused now. "What do you mean? Was she taken away?"

"Elizabeth never told me what happened," he finally admitted. "She never told me what she did with our daughter." He grimaced, remembering something horrible.

Rose rushed to his side. "What is it, Edmond?"

"A year before Elizabeth became pregnant again, I found her in the graveyard."

Rose didn't like where this was going, but still asked, "What was she doing?"

Edmond continued. "The snow was coming down heavy, and she was on her hands and knees. Everything was like ice; I still remember the coat she was wearing. And as I walked closer to her, I noticed she was digging up our son's grave."

Rose brought her hand to her mouth.

"I was so horrified that I thought I was dreaming. I didn't want to believe that Elizabeth was capable of doing such a thing. So I ran to her and pulled her back. She screamed at me to let her go, but I wouldn't—not until she calmed herself.

Elizabeth kicked at Edmond as she wailed. "I want my son back!"

Edmond held Elizabeth back. "Our son is gone. You have to accept that, Elizabeth."

Elizabeth went limp in Edmond's arms, and finally he let her go. She sobbed and rocked back and forth. She was covered in snow and dirt from trying to dig up the grave.

"Tell me what I need to do to make it easier for you." Edmond said. He begged her to give him a way out of this madness. "I miss him, too, but this can't go on, Elizabeth. It has to stop, so tell me what I need to do."

"No," Elizabeth said quietly.

Edmond leaned in. "What?"

Elizabeth spoke louder this time. "No. This isn't real."

Edmond ignored her words, "Elizabeth, I need you to tell me how I can help you."

Finally, Elizabeth looked up at him, her face stained with tears, her eyes dilated. "Why can't I have a life that is my own?"

Edmond didn't know what to say to her; instead he picked her up and carried her back into the mansion. He ordered Thackeray to get a bath ready in their room and helped Elizabeth get undressed. Her body went limp, and she would do nothing for herself. It was up to Edmond to clean the dirt from under her fingernails and wash her.

That was the first time Edmond ever truly felt distant from her.

"Elizabeth," Edmond said, "talk to me, please."

"I want another," she told him, eventually looking his way.

Edmond was confused. "Another?"

Elizabeth stood up, water dripping from her body. "I want another child."

Edmond wasn't sure what to say. If they had another child, and it also died, he wasn't sure if he could keep on living. "Are you sure?" he asked.

"Yes." Elizabeth grabbed a towel off the floor and dried herself. "I need you to leave. Don't come back in the room until I say so," she ordered.

Edmond was taken aback by her forceful words but did as he was told and did not return until early the next morning. He found Elizabeth asleep in the bed. The water in the tin tub was cold and milky white from the soap, and the fireplace had resorted to ashes. A stifling cold winter wind had found its way in through a partially opened window, along with some snow. Edmond was quick to shut the window and latch it. He lay down next to Elizabeth. Her body was cold, but that didn't seem to bother her.

Elizabeth eventually woke up to find Edmond rubbing her back to warm her. "I'm sorry," she said.

Edmond softly hushed her. "No, I'm sorry for putting you in this mess." And he kissed her cold forehead.

When Edmond finished speaking, he looked at Rose and slid a stray hair behind her ear. He then noticed the light from the sun poking its way into the mansion. "I think it be best if you stayed home today, Rose."

"Why?" she asked.

"I need some time to myself."

Teasing, Rose responded, "You have nothing but time, Edmond."

Edmond smiled. "Not as much time as you may think," he said. "Go home and spend time with your parents today and the next, and the day after that, if need be."

Rose raised a brow. "Are you trying to get rid of me?" she joked.

This time Edmond laughed. "I assure I am not, no." He stood and helped Rose to her feet. "The days that you will be gone will go by quickly, you'll see." He opened the door leading outside, and there was Thackeray reading a book. Edmond cleared his throat. "Thackeray, would you be ever so kind enough to walk Miss Rose home?"

Thackeray closed his book with a thump and jumped to his feet. "Of course, but why must she leave so soon?"

Rose intervened. "Edmond wants me to spend the next couple of days with my parents. Don't worry, Thackeray. It'll go by fast," she assured him.

Thackeray nodded. He had no doubt that Rose would return soon. He picked up a brown leather bag and threw it over his shoulders. "Shall we go, then?" Thackeray said and took her hand.

Midway between the house and the mansion, Thackeray stopped and tugged at Rose's sleeve.

"What's the matter?" she asked.

Thackeray rummaged through his leather bag and pulled out a pale-blue leather journal. "Take it. It was Elizabeth's."

Rose was almost too scared to touch it. "No, I can't," she protested.

Thackeray pushed the journal into her hands. "Elizabeth left it in my care, and it would mean a lot to me if you took it. It would mean a lot to Elizabeth, too. You deserve to know how she felt." Thackeray paused. "You're the first person I have become friends with in the last two hundred years. This has to mean something. I also marked an entry that I want you to read first."

Rose looked down at the journal. It was smooth. "I don't know what to say, Thackeray."

Thackeray wasted no time. "Just tell me that you'll read it," he said.

Rose nodded. "Yes, of course. Does Edmond know you have this?"

Thackeray shook his head. "No, I could never bring myself to give it to him. The words within those pages will sting you more than what Edmond has told you, I assure you." He threw his bag over his shoulder again. "Shall we keep going?"

As Rose made it back into the house, her parents' alarm clock was going off. She had returned just in time.

A yawn erupted from her as she rubbed her tired eyes after a nearly sleepless night. She headed upstairs to her room and collapsed on her bed. There she stared at Elizabeth's diary before finally opening it. The writing was neat, and the paper barely showed its age. Thackeray had done a good job keeping the journal intact.

Rose opened the journal to the page Thackeray had marked and began reading.

1880, 9th of July,

Dear diary,

I must admit I am terribly unhappy. If I could turn back time, I would have never chosen this life. Don't worry; I love my Edmond with all my heart, but a life such as this is not worth living. My name, as you know, dear diary, is Elizabeth Ann Gray. Long before this happened, I saw myself growing old with my husband and being surrounded by my children and grandchildren. But you see I am unable to grow old. Why, you may be wondering? I'm immortal. It's such a silly word when others think of it to be in only story books, but it's real outside of them as well.

I've been living here in the Valcain mansion for the last hundred years, a place people have no desire to seek out, or they have forgotten about us entirely. I have been with child twice in all my long years, and even though it may seem I have all the time in the world to do whatever it is I please or go wherever I want, there is a catch to this immortality: I cannot venture far from the forest in which the mansion resides. Edmond has told me that it has something to do with the plants he used to make the potion. We have tried growing more elsewhere, but they die within a week, so we are grounded to this forest as the roots are to the trees. If I go too far, my skin turns gray and wrinkly. I do not know what would happen if I went too far, but the idea is truly fascinating.

Something else I must admit is that nine years ago I gave away my three-month-old daughter. I was walking with her in the forest one morning as I often did and came across two hunters. I felt no ill will coming from them, so I did what I thought was best for my daughter: I gave her to the older huntsman. I practically forced him to take her. And when he tried to give her back, I told him that I was incapable of taking care of her, that I was dying from consumption, and there was no one else I could turn to. Before I left I told them that her name was Elizabeth. Giving her my name was the least I could do for her, and besides that, I didn't want her living my life. I wanted her to be free.

The huntsmen came after me, but I know this forest well and lost them easily. I know Edmond is having a difficult time forgiving me, but surely he must understand that what I did was for the best.

The reason I am even explaining this is not to satisfy my own thoughts and peace of mind, but to leave proof of the life I lived and reasoning behind my actions. And there is another reason why I write this: just last week I saw a child in the forest. She was well dressed and wore her hair in a messy braid. When she saw me, she looked startled, and I smiled, trying to ease any worries she might have had. I was compelled to speak with her and asked if she was lost, but she shook her head. And when

I asked for her name, she told me it was Elizabeth. I started crying right away; I was so happy.

My little Elizabeth was alive and healthy, and she looked so happy. I wanted to say more to her, but a voice called out to her and she turned and ran up to the man I had given her to all those years ago. My heart was filled with joy. He had kept her and raised her as his own.

Papa, she called him. I nearly started sobbing. And then he asked me if we had ever met, but I told him no, of course, that I was just passing through to pick some berries, and we said our goodbyes. I will live vicariously through my daughter; to know that she is living a normal life makes me feel at ease.

It is decided then: I will leave this place with or without Edmond and Thackeray. I have to know what happens. I've been wondering what lies beyond this forest lately.

Rose closed the diary after finishing the entry and rubbed her tired eyes again. There was still more to read, but she could no longer force herself to look at the pages. She knew so much about Edmond and Elizabeth, but there was still so much that she didn't know about Thackeray.

For such a little boy he had much to tell.

Chapter Seven

Rose did as Edmond had instructed: stay away from the manor and spend the next few days with her parents. Even Rose thought it was a good idea. She had forgotten how fun her parents could be without all the stress and work at home.

The three revisited London to do more shopping and catch up with more of Luke and Tiffany's friends from their college days. They were told that visiting the art museum would be worth their time and money, so they did.

Rose was nervous about going, wondering if she would find anything referring to the mansion.

Of course, she was mesmerized by everything the museum had to offer and often tuned out the tour guide speaking while she concentrated on a specific painting or statue. One particular painting drew her complete concentration.

The painting was of a young woman, maybe in her early twenties. The woman was holding a paint brush, with an easel beside her. To Rose it looked as if the woman was trying to paint herself. She admired her long, blond wavy hair and blue eyes and the way she held herself. Rose was almost jealous of her beauty. Her plain blue dress, nothing spectacular, made her porcelain white skin and natural beauty stand out.

Rose scanned the plaque at the bottom of the painting. It read: unfinished, eighteen-hundreds. Rose glanced back up at the painting and found it hard to believe that it was unfinished. She thought it was perfect. Rose snapped a photo of it, then quickly tucked her phone back into her jeans pocket and hurried to catch up with the group. The crowd was gathering around a glass-encased painting the guide stood next to.

"Why is it behind a glass case and not out in the open like the rest of the paintings?" one woman asked.

"The painting was found exposed to too many elements and was greatly damage," the tour guide explained. "Unfortunately, we have to keep it sealed tight in here so nothing else may damage it."

"Who painted it?" asked another visitor.

"The name of the painter is unknown," the guide responded. "However, we have an idea as to when it was painted, and the answer to that is mid-seventeenth century. We are currently looking into the identity of the painters dating to that era. We only recently found this wonderful masterpiece, so there is still little we know of it."

The painting was of a young boy, maybe five or six, sitting in an oversized red-cushioned chair. His wavy blond hair was trimmed neatly to his chin. His jacket was a deep red with black buttons, his breeches were black, and his long white socks rested beneath shiny black dress shoes. Draped over his shoulders was a white animal fur, and in his right hand he held a tall wooden cane that glistened. A maroon sheet stretched behind him from where he was seated all the way to the floor.

The markings on the legs of a piano off to the side looked familiar to Rose. Of course! How could she forget that beautiful design? Rose had seen it at the mansion.

Just as the guide said, the painting had been damaged. Age spots were visible in every corner of the painting, and exposure to the sun had faded much of it. When the group walked off, Rose sneaked a photo of the painting, barely pulling her phone out of her pocket.

While Rose continued on the tour, enjoying the rest of the sights, she couldn't help but think back to the painting of the boy. The secret of the mansion was in her hands. She could tell anyone about it, let them in on the secret, have her five minutes of fame, but Rose dared not. She kept her mouth shut. The idea of telling others was simply absurd to her. This secret was Edmond's, Thackeray's and hers, and it would remain that way. She wasn't about to spoil that. To Rose it was such an honor to be welcomed back to the mansion and trusted by the others.

That evening, just before sunset, Rose sat in the living room with her parents and watched the news. A rattle at the windows made her glance up, but she soon turned her attention back to the television.

There was talk about a storm heading their way, but with the way the wind shook the windows, it didn't seem like anything not to worry about.

"We should have gone shopping for food before coming back," said Tiffany. "What if we get shut in for the next couple of days because the roads are closed? We'll go hungry."

Lucas shrugged. "There is plenty of food in the fridge. We'll be fine."

Tiffany got up to double-check and was not happy about what she found.

"There are a few pizzas and some water and milk, but we're nearly out of bread and cheese," she told her husband.

Lucas sighed and turned down the volume on the television before turning to his wife. "Are you suggesting we make a quick trip to the grocery store?"

Tiffany was quick to grab the car keys. "Why not. The store is ten minutes away. We'll go in and out real quickly." She looked to Rose. "Do you want to come?"

"No, thanks," said Rose. "I'll stay here."

"Maybe that's best," Lucas said. "She can keep an eye on the house."

Rose wasn't sure if it was such a great idea to stay there alone, but the idea of driving out into a storm didn't thrill her either. She sat on the couch staring at the television but not really paying attention to it. Her mind was fixated on the noises outside. The loud whistling of the wind sounded like wild animals to her, and the darkening sky was foreboding.

The sounds grew louder by the minute, and it seemed as if her parents had been gone forever, though only ten minutes had passed. They should be back soon, she thought.

Suddenly, the television turned off and the lights went out as lightning struck somewhere close. Rose pulled her legs up to her chest and hugged them, counting until she heard the thunder again. She barely got to five before lightning struck again, this time right outside the window. The room flashed, and Rose dropped to the floor, covering her face.

As one last thunder clap roared across the sky, another lightning bolt hit somewhere close. A tree fell, breaking the two front windows. Rain and wind rushed into the house, and Rose took shelter behind the couch. She was too scared to move, only scream and cry.

Finally, she picked herself up and ran into the kitchen to use the phone, but it was dead. Rose cursed and ran up to her bedroom only to find that a falling branch had broken a window. The covers on her bed were wet, and so was a pile of her dirty clothes. She closed the door to her room and ran to her parents', but there was a giant leak in the roof over their room, too, and Rose was too scared to stay there, afraid that the ceiling might collapse. The whole house, in fact, sounded as if it would cave in on itself.

In the end Rose was left with no other choice. She didn't want to be stuck at the house alone in a raging storm. And where were her parents? Were they holed up at the store, or had they driven into a ditch? The very idea made Rose's skin crawl, and she made up her mind: she would go to the mansion. She slipped on her boots and ran out of the house and into the storm.

Meanwhile, Edmond sat in his chair in his room in front of the fireplace reading a book. To his side was a glass of wine, which he occasionally took sips from. He looked up from his book long enough to gaze out the window and watch the wrath of the storm. With a heavy sigh and a sip of wine, he returned to reading. Edmond had grown used to violent storms, as had Thackeray.

Despite their simple life, the two had enjoyed the thrill of a violent tempest. Seeing as they had been virtually forgotten by the rest of the world, they never had any real disturbances or threats, at least until Rose. She knew of their existence but accepted them for who they were.

Edmond's lips curled into a smile as thoughts of Rose filled his mind. He stood up and closed his book, placing it atop of the fireplace, and tossed the remainder of his wine into the fire. The sound of the liquid sizzling in the flames was soothing. He leaned forward, resting his hands on the stone of the fireplace, and looked into the flames. Memories of the past enveloped his mind like a heavy fog. Edmond could still hear the voices and see the faces of those who died that fateful night. Living his life the way he had was one way, Edmond told himself, that he would not let their deaths be in vain. As long as there was still breath in his lungs, he would continue to live for all the lives lost.

Edmond pulled himself away from the fireplace and opened his bedroom door. The hallway was cool and dark with small candles to light the way for him. The storm could still be seen through the cracks in the curtains. He made his way to the great room and found another fire lit. Thackeray was lying on the sofa, nibbling on a bone from supper.

Thackeray sensed Edmond standing there and sat up to greet him.

"It's an exciting night," he said as Edmond took a seat next to him.

"Hmm, indeed it is," said Edmond, looking over at his longtime friend. "Still hungry, I see. Didn't get enough for supper?"

It was rare to hear Edmond make a joke. He always felt that he had to be formal and respectful, but when it came to Thackeray, he tried to be more laid back.

At that moment the front doors swung open, the storm-driven wind making the flames in the fireplace dance crazily. There stood Rose, soaking wet from head to toe and shivering uncontrollably.

Edmond rushed to her aid, picking her up bridal style and guiding her to a sofa next to the fireplace. He grabbed a blanket and draped it over her while Thackeray locked the front doors.

Edmond could hardly speak, he was so taken aback by Rose's appearance. "What in God's name were you doing out in the storm? You could have gotten seriously hurt."

Rose wrapped the blanket more tightly around her. "I'm sorry, but my parents left to go to the store to get more food before the storm, but it hit before they came back. I'm worried they're stuck somewhere, and I didn't want to be alone in the house. Branches were breaking in through the windows. I got scared!" She looked wide-eyed at Edmond and Thackeray as she said this.

Edmond gave her a gentle smile. "You silly girl," he said, stroking her cold cheek. "At least you are safe now." He then noticed she was caked in mud from the waist down. "Come," he said. "Let's get you cleaned up." He picked her up again, but this time Rose protested.

"You don't have to carry me, Edmond."

"Of course, I do. A respectable man takes good care of a respectable woman."

Rose blushed at this. "You forget that we are from two completely different times."

Edmond raised a brow. "And that should change this situation how?" He gave her a wry smile.

All Rose could do was smile back; she knew she had lost this debate.

When they reached Edmond's room, he put Rose down and turned to Thackeray. "Will you help me prepare a hot bath for Rose?"

"My pleasure," Thackeray said.

"Go ahead of me then," said Edmond. "I'm going to show Rose where the clean clothes are."

Thackeray left, closing the door behind him.

Rose looked at Edmond as he opened a walk-in closet. "He's very loyal, you know," said Rose.

Edmond didn't respond except to bring out a white nightgown and bathrobe. "If you want something else to wear, everything you'll need will be on the bottom," he said, tossing the garments on the bed. "Yes, I know he is," Edmond finally responded, "and I am very grateful to him; perhaps more so than he knows." Rose said nothing. Edmond looked to her, "Feel free to change behind the privacy wall. I should go help Thackeray." With that, Edmond left the room.

Rose took her time undressing, knowing how the others frequently came back and forth with buckets of water to heat over the fire. It took at least an hour for them to prepare a bath for Rose, but she gladly sat in Edmond's chair and waited.

"Here is everything else that you'll need," said Thackeray as he placed a towel and a bar of soap on the floor next to the tub.

"Thanks, Thackeray." She gave him a small kiss on the forehead. "Thank you both."

Edmond and Thackeray left Rose to take her bath. The water was just the right temperature. Rose let her aching body soak for a long time before taking the soap and washing the grime from her skin. She saw no point in washing her hair, because it was already partially wet from the storm.

When she finished her bath, she took the towel Thackeray had given her and dried every inch of her body before putting the nightgown on. She then poked her head out from the room and looked to find Edmond sitting on the floor by himself. "Where is Thackeray?" she asked.

"He went to bed," Edmond answered as he stood up and walked back to his room and Rose followed.

"Thanks again, Edmond," Rose said.

Edmond gave her a small bow. "It was nothing, truly. It's always a pleasure to help you, Rose." He was going to say more but was startled when Rose wrapped her arms around him. "Honestly, Rose," Edmond started. "There is no need to thank me. I'm just glad you're safe."

Rose smothered her face in his chest. "But you're so kind to me, you and Thackeray. I've never met such nice people before."

Edmond smiled. "Rose, what we do is common sense. We don't do this because we're told to or because we want something out of it. We do it because it's the right thing to do. Besides, we like you."

Sighing, Rose let go of Edmond and made her way to the bed.

The flickering light from the fireplace was now dimming.

Edmond walked over to the edge of the bed, the dim light casting shadows all over his body as he leaned against the bedpost. He looked like a dark, gallant prince.

Rose crawled across the bed to Edmond and put her arms around him once again.

Edmond's first thought was to push Rose away from him, but he stood there still. He wasn't sure if he should hug Rose back, seeing how he didn't want her to get the wrong idea. Or perhaps the wrong idea was the right idea. Edmond didn't know what to do. He had known Rose for only two months, but already he was growing close to her. He finally gave in to his emotions and put his arms around Rose's waist. "Rose?" he said softly.

"Hmm."

"I think you should lie down. You've had a rough night, and you need your rest. You're not thinking clearly."

Rose moved back but still held on to him. "But Edmond, I am thinking very clearly."

"I think not." Edmond pushed her away and made her lie down.

"Are you unhappy with me, Edmond?" Rose asked suddenly.

"No," said Edmond, taking a seat next to her on the bed. "Just a little confused."

"Confused?" she asked.

Edmond found it hard to spit the words out. "You're acting as if we are lovers."

Rose brushed her face against the feather pillow. "That seems nice," she murmured dreamily.

Edmond let the conversation go. He noticed Rose was shivering, so he held her under the covers and rubbed her hands between his.

Just then, Edmond stopped, realizing that she had fallen asleep, and chuckled to himself. She looked even more innocent now. Her cheeks were rosy red, her long eyelashes casting shadows on her cheeks, and her lips curved in a cutesy smile.

Edmond's eyes were locked on her. He couldn't help but look at her. She reminded him so much of Elizabeth. Yes, his sweet Elizabeth. And like that he bent down and softly kissed her.

Rose suddenly held him down, keeping him there to deepen the kiss.

When she finally let go, Edmond didn't know what to do. She had tricked him, but he wasn't upset. "Why?" he asked.

Rose smiled up at him. "It had to happen sooner or later, didn't it?" Her sweet smile turned devious.

Edmond leaned in for a kiss, making it longer and sweeter. Edmond soon lay beside Rose holding her and continuing to give her sweet kisses. And then, quite suddenly, he stopped.

"What's wrong?" asked Rose.

Edmond sat up, touching his lips as he enjoyed the feel and taste of Rose. "I'm worried that if we continue, it may turn into something else." Rose gave him a pouty look, but he wasn't about to give in. "Come," he said. "Let us sleep." He lay back down facing her but did not touch her.

Rose was not shy about snuggling up next to Edmond. She rested her forehead on his chest and closed her eyes, listening to the raging storm outside. Why did it have to turn out like this, thought Rose. I finally found someone I really like, and this is what happens. Rose knew she was digging herself a deeper hole with every passing day that she was here. She adored Edmond and Thackeray and always wanted to be their friend. It was going to be difficult to leave, but if she were to stay? No, she thought, I can't do that. But what if it was possible? Oh, the possibilities!

Rose pushed the idea from her thoughts and decided to forget about it for the time being.

The following morning Edmond was not there when Rose awoke. She placed her hand on his side of the bed, but it was cold. He must have gotten up way before her.

As she rubbed her face and stretched, she stood and walked over to check her clothes. They were dry save for her jeans, and she didn't feel like wearing them while they were damp. Feeling curious, she walked over to Edmond's closet and stepped inside. There was a mix of men's and women's clothes, letting Rose know that Edmond and Elizabeth shared a closet.

Rose looked through the dresses and chose one that looked simple to put on. It was a plain blue cotton dress with faded pink flowers and white ruffles. The sleeves were three-quarter length, and the fabric was so light that it was perfect for a summer day. She then grabbed a petticoat to match the dress and a white strapless slip to wear underneath. She even found a pair of matching blue slip-on flats.

When Rose finished dressing, she looked at herself in the mirror, oohing and aahing over her appearance. She had wanted to do something with her hair but had nothing to put it up or pin it back.

Rose left to find the others and, venturing outside, spotted Edmond in his garden.

When Edmond heard his name, he stopped what he was doing and looked to see Rose running toward him. He was so mesmerized by her looks that he was speechless. "Good morning, Rose," he managed to say. "Where did you get the dress?" He knew where she had gotten it, but he felt the need to ask anyway.

Rose looked at him sheepishly. "I found it in your closet. I'll take it off, if you want me to."

Edmond shook his head. "No, no. That is fine. The dress looks lovely on you."

Rose blushed.

Edmond cleared his throat. "Have you eaten yet?"

"I haven't, but I'm not really hungry. I'll wait for the next meal to eat," she replied. "By the way, where is Thackeray?"

Edmond pointed to his left. "He's gone fishing. Elizabeth and he always fished together. It was their favorite hobby to do together. I'm sure Thackeray would love it if you joined him."

Rose nodded to this. "On the west side of the river then," she said. "I'll be able to find him if I just walk straight, right?" she asked.

Edmond smiled and kissed her forehead. "Yes."

Rose walked for maybe fifteen minutes before she came to the river and found Thackeray standing a few yards away. He was casting his line, trying to get the perfect arc to land his bait in just the right spot. He was an excellent fisherman.

As Rose made her way toward him, the earth crunched beneath her feet.

Thackeray glanced at her and then looked back at the river. "It's about time you showed up, Elizabeth. I was beginning to think...." He stopped himself and looked back at Rose. "Oh, Rose, it's you. Forgive me."

Rose stood beside him now. "For what?"

"For calling you by the wrong name."

Rose looked at him sympathetically. "It's okay to miss her, Thackeray."

He said nothing.

"Look," began Rose, "you can tell me anything. I've kept your secret about the mansion, haven't I?" She placed a hand on his shoulder to comfort him.

Thackeray bent down and put his fishing rod in a holder he had made. "Do you ever feel like someone is watching you, even if you are completely alone?" he asked.

Rose knelt beside him. "What are you trying to say, Thackeray?"

He took a deep breath. "Sometimes it feels like Elizabeth is still here."

"Of course, she is," Rose said, pointing to Thackeray's heart.

Thackeray shook his head. "I don't mean it like that."

"Then explain it to me."

Thackeray fiddled with his thumbs, contemplating what to say. "Sometimes I see Elizabeth in the forest. When I run after her, she always leads me near the edge of the forest, and I can never follow her after that. I want to go with her, but I know I can't leave Edmond behind."

"Are you sure it's Elizabeth you see?" Rose asked.

"Who else would it be?" he said.

This time Rose shook her head. "No, what I mean is, are you sure what you're seeing is real?" She felt silly for saying this, considering she had seen Elizabeth's ghost herself.

Thackeray looked almost offended.

Rose was quick to apologize. "I'm sorry, but don't you think it's a little scary?"

"Scary?"

Rose nodded.

"I can't say that it is," he replied. "Have you seen or heard anything weird? I mean, you are staying in her old home."

Rose decided to be honest with him. "I think I have seen her."

Thackeray was pleased to hear this and smiled. "Good, I'm glad."

"Has Edmond seen her?" she asked suddenly.

Thackeray picked up his rod and gently pulled on it. "If he has, he certainly hasn't told me anything about it."

"You haven't asked him?" Rose asked, sounding surprised.

Thackeray was amused by this. "My dear Rose, there are things better left unsaid, especially when it comes to Edmond. There are things I will never tell him. I know he has his secrets, and I have mine."

Curious now, Rose asked, "Why don't you want to tell him, Thackeray?"

"When Elizabeth gave me her diary, she told me to read all of it. She also told me never to let Edmond see it. If you've read the entry I told you about, then you can understand why Elizabeth never wanted Edmond to read her thoughts. I'm not sure he'd be able to live with himself."

Rose was trying hard to understand. "I've only read the entry you told me about, unfortunately."

Thackeray took in a deep breath. "Then you know that she gave her baby away to hunters." He paused. "Elizabeth never told Edmond what she did with their child because she knew what he would do."

"He'd go after the child," Rose cut in.

Thackeray nodded. "Precisely," he thought for a moment, remembering the past. "They argued for days about it. I didn't think there would ever be an end, and as I sat and watched it all happen, I knew everything that was going on. I knew Edmond's side, and I knew Elizabeth's side. I felt sorry for both of them."

Just then, Thackeray's rod tip snapped downward, and he pulled a fish in with one strong tug. Rose watched in amazement as the fish went flying out of the river.

Thackeray was quick to catch it and place it in a tin bucket filled with water.

"You're really good at fishing." Rose praised him, trying to change the subject

"It's all I seem to do these days, so, of course, I've gotten really good at it. Thank you though. I appreciate it." He handed Rose his fishing rod and picked up the bucket filled with fish. "Should we head back?"

Rose smiled. "Yeah, let's go home."

As they made their way back, Rose stopped for a moment. She could have sworn she heard something or someone.

"Rose, are you coming?" Thackeray called out to her.

Rose turned her attention to Thackeray and hurried to his side. "Yeah, sorry."

They walked back in silence, listening to the whimpering sound of the wind. This time, though, it sounded different.

Chapter Eight

It was still the same day after the night of the storm. Rose was sitting outside with Edmond and Thackeray eating fish for lunch. The wet grass smelled nice, and there was a cool breeze, though the sun kept the temperature comfortable.

"What a nice day," said Thackeray with a smile while sipping his tea.

Rose was happy to see him smiling. After what he had told her, she was worried about him and how he felt. She knew that he wasn't a little boy, that underneath that cute smile and curly brown hair was someone who had lived at least three lifetimes.

Rose lay back on the blanket that had been set out for their lunch and looked up at the clear sky. There didn't seem to be any sign of a storm today. She was glad for that. But as she stretched, taking a deep breath, she suddenly gasped and sat up.

"What's the matter?" asked Edmond.

"My parents!" She quickly stood and headed inside the mansion.

Edmond and Thackeray were quick to follow. The plates and cups could be picked up later.

"Rose, what's wrong with your parents?" Edmond asked, following her to his bedroom.

Rose swung the bedroom door open. "The storm wrecked the house, and if my parents come back and see that I'm not there, they will freak out." She walked over to her clothes to check if they were dry. "I need to go back now." She grabbed her clothes and changed behind the divider as quickly as she could.

"That is a problem," said Thackeray, standing in the doorway. "I do hope they're okay."

Rose stepped out from behind the divider and slipped on her shoes. "I'm sorry to leave like this."

Edmond shook his head and said: "No, it's perfectly fine. I hope everything will be all right."

"I'll come back as soon as I can, I promise," Rose said, giving Edmond a peck on the cheek and hugging Thackeray goodbye.

The peck on the cheek surprised Thackeray, but he said nothing about it.

"Rose," Edmond suddenly called out.

Rose turned, looking impatient.

"You can keep the dress, if you like." He picked it up and handed it to her.

"Are you sure?"

Edmond nodded. "Who else is going to wear it? Of course I'm sure."

Rose wished she could have stayed longer, but she knew she had to go. "I'll see you both again soon. Bye!"

When Rose was gone, Thackeray looked up at Edmond with crossed arms. "What was that all about," he asked. "What happened between you and Rose last night?"

Edmond said nothing as he walked toward the bedroom door, a grin on his face.

"Master?"

Edmond ignored Thackeray's prompt, saying only, "Feel free to do whatever you please for the rest of the day." He was in a daze now; that much was obvious to Thackeray.

For someone who knew about almost everything, Thackeray was left dumbfounded and lost in thought, though it had occurred to him that perhaps those two were realizing their feelings for each other.

Edmond told him that he could spend the rest of the day as he saw fit, which meant no chores. Thackeray's first plan of action was to read or play the piano, for he always spent his free time reading or in the music room. Rarely did he get a chance to enjoy the sun on his skin. He was always too busy gardening or hunting to enjoy his time outside.

Thackeray ran to his room to grab a kite he had made. His room was simple: a single bed with dark sheets laid unmade and wooden toys and books spread out on the floor. The curtains had long since withered away, so the room was filled with sunshine.

As he made his way out behind the mansion, Thackeray waited for a generous breeze and let his kite fly as high as it could without tangling in the branches. Sunlight streamed through the leaves, casting shadowy images. But when the wind began to whip around, he lost his grip, and the kite took off further back in the yard. He ran his fastest, trying to keep up, but stopped abruptly when he realized where the kite had landed.

The graveyard was just a few feet away. Recollections of the past haunted him as he looked back to see if Edmond was around, but he was nowhere to be seen. If Thackeray wanted his kite back, he would have to go in and get it himself. He wasn't a child anymore and couldn't expect Edmond to take care of every little problem he faced.

Thackeray reluctantly stepped into the graveyard, his shoes crunching the earth as he tiptoed. He bent down to pick up his kite, and suddenly a hand popped out of the ground and grabbed his arm. As Thackeray pulled away, a boy came ripping out of the ground, his skin peeling off and his eyes white.

"Help us, Thackeray!" the boy yelled.

Thackeray managed to free himself from the boy's grasp, but now he was covered with ashes. He tried to brush them off his body, but it was in vain. He was smothered in them, and more was piling on top of him. Thackeray tripped over his feet trying to escape and had to crawl his way out with one hand clutching the kite.

When he was free, he turned around, but there was no boy there and no ashes. Thackeray had imagined it all. Tears poured from his eyes as he tried not to think about the past. Perhaps that was why he always kept himself busy, never wanting the past to creep up on him. All those screams of the ones who had perished in the massacre had sullied his mind. He was sorry that he couldn't save them and wished that he could have died with them.

Angry, Thackeray threw his kite to the ground, buried his face in his hands, and sobbed. That nightmarish day was all coming back to him. He remembered running through the halls, trying to find a safe place to hide. Little Thackeray never told anyone—not even Elizabeth—what had happened to him that night. He was caught and dragged out with the rest of the boys and girls and thrown into a pit of fire. Kicking and screaming did him no good, as his hands and feet were bound. He cried out for Edmond to save him, but Edmond never showed up. He didn't even know where Elizabeth was.

"Demon child," they yelled at him. "Go to hell!"

As he was dragged to his death, he could hear them cursing his existence and calling him names—monster, witch, demon, devil, imp—as he was hurled into the flames. He could feel his skin melting from his body, his clothing turning to ash, and his hair withering away. Thackeray witnessed a boy wailing before he was blinded, and Thackeray took his hands and held them until the boy's cries subsided and his white skin blackened and blistered. Thackeray wanted to tell the boy how sorry he was, but his voice was lost, his throat destroyed by the heat and smoke.

Suddenly, Thackeray lost consciousness, and when he awoke, the flames had died down and the screams had subsided. The air felt cold now as he lay upon the soiled pile of bodies. He was the only one to have survived. And as he looked down at his hands, he watched as they and the rest of his body miraculously healed in a flash. Even his hair grew back.

Thackeray pulled himself up from the pit, naked and scared.

Snow fell hard, putting out whatever flames had reached the mansion. There was blood and bodies everywhere. Thackeray grabbed a blanket off the floor and wrapped himself in it. Everything was quiet, save for the heavy snow that blew in through the broken windows.

He stopped short when he saw Edmond lying on the floor. He had been stabbed multiple times but was waking up, looking disoriented as bodies littered the floor around him.

Elizabeth came running down the stairs, calling out to them. When she saw Thackeray, she embraced him and asked if he was all right. Of course, he wasn't okay, but he would never tell her that, and he just nodded.

Now, Thackeray bit down on his tongue, drawing blood, as he woke himself from this feverish nightmare. The images were no more, and his mind was clear. He thought of Rose and how happy she made him and wondered what it would be like if she lived forever. Thackeray wiped the tears from his eyes and picked himself up. Playing the piano seemed like a good idea.

Rose made it back to the house within a reasonable time and kicked off her muddy boots as she walked through the back door. As she placed the dress on the table, the front door squeaked as it was opened. She walked into the living room and saw her parents' horrified looks.

"Are you okay?" Tiffany asked as she ran up to her daughter and gave her a quick hug.

"Yeah, I'm fine. I stayed in the basement for most of the night."

Lucas walked around the room stunned. "I'm surprised the whole place didn't fall down."

"I'm sorry we couldn't make it home till now. The grocery store wouldn't let us leave." Tiffany apologized multiple times as she checked Rose for any scratches.

Lucas walked into the kitchen to make a phone call, but the line was dead. "We'll have to drive to Alan and Diana's place. We can't stay here. I'll make some phone calls when we get there so we can get the house fixed."

"How far away do they live?" Rose asked.

"About fifteen or twenty minutes from here," Tiffany replied.

Rose slouched. "How long will we stay there?" She didn't want to be away from the mansion long.

"As long as it takes to get this place fixed," her father answered. "Why? You seem a little disappointed."

Rose shrugged. "I like this place is all."

Addressing the two, Tiffany said: "Let's get our things packed and head over to Alan and Diana's, okay? Hopefully, we'll be back here before we have to go home."

Rose's heart sank. She didn't want to stay with Alan and Diana for the remainder of her stay in England. How would she make it to the mansion? It would take her four times as long if she walked, and she didn't want to take a bus or have a taxi drop her off at the house. She felt like running to the mansion to tell Edmond and Thackeray the news, but she knew she didn't have time and instead walked up stairs to pack her things.

Alan and Diana lived in a small neighborhood with a fenced-in yard. A small dog barked at them from behind a window as Rose and her parents made their way to the front door and rang the bell.

Diana was there to greet them and looked puzzled when she saw their luggage. "What happened?" she asked, stepping aside.

"The house had some damage done to it by the storm. We would have called but the line is down," Lucas explained. "We were hoping to stay here until it's fixed. Sorry for intruding like this."

Diana was quick to make space in the living room. There was no need, though, the house was large, and the living room was spacious enough to fit at least fifteen people comfortably.

"Alan is at work right now. I was just getting supper together." Diana said. "We have an extra room upstairs and a living area in the basement." Looking at Rose, she said. "The couches down there are very comfy."

Rose carried her luggage to the basement and was not disappointed by what she saw. As Diana said, the basement was large, and the couches more than adequate. A flat-screen television hung on a wall with three remotes sitting on a glass coffee table. A dart board hung on the opposite wall along with some workout equipment and standing off to the side was a small bar and a tiny metal fireplace. Perhaps staying there wouldn't be so bad, Rose thought. Still, she wanted to make it back to the mansion as soon as possible.

Random portraits were displayed throughout the house. Some were of Diana and Alan and the rest of their family, while others were of their ancestors. One in particular was a man with short, slicked-back black hair. The dreary look in his eyes sent a shiver down Rose's spine, as did his black suit.

Another portrait was of a young man with black hair combed to one side. Standing next to him was an older woman and man; Rose guessed they were the young man's parents. They all bore the same dull expression, and Rose wondered if no one was ever happy back in the nineteenth century.

All the commotion taking place had taken its toll on Rose. She set her luggage aside and lay down on the couch. She could smell supper and tried to guess what it was. Maybe steak, but it could have been tacos. Either sounded delicious.

As Rose snuggled among the throw pillows, she drifted off to sleep. She dreamed of standing in a fog-shrouded field with a tall, slender man a few feet away, his back to her. He slowly turned, his long, thinned-out black hair tied back, and his nose long and crooked, and clasped his long, bony hands. It was the man from the portrait with the black suit. A sinister look spread upon his face as he stared coldly at Rose, his thin, pale lips curving into a smile and his deep-green eyes flashing. The entirety of his outfit was black, making him look like a crypt keeper. He opened his mouth to speak, but no words came out.

Rose felt herself sinking, and when she opened her eyes she was on the floor.

"Ouch," she said into the carpet.

Just then her mother called down to her, telling her that supper was ready. Rose was glad about this and ran upstairs. Alan was home, and everyone was grabbing a plate. The meal was steak tacos.

Everyone gathered round the table, and the banter began in earnest.

"I can't believe you still live in this old house," Lucas said.

Diana shrugged as she poured herself a glass of wine. "Why not? The place is paid for. We only have to worry about the electricity and water…besides other expenses like the internet and our phones."

"And it's in a good neighborhood," Alan added.

Looking up from her plate, Rose asked, "Who built the house?"

Diana was more than pleased to tell her. "His name was Viktor Slater. He built this home back in the mid-seventeen-hundreds, if I remember correctly. He was my great-great-great-great-grandfather."

Rose's eyes grew twice their size. "That's a lot of greats."

Diana laughed, then sighed. "Nobody knows what happened to him though."

Alan wriggled in the chair, as if he knew what was coming next and wanted to make sure he was comfortable.

"What do you mean?" asked Rose.

Diana shrugged. "That's the thing, no one knows. Not even the family closest to him knew what happened. There is talk that he went into the Epping Forest and killed himself after his supposed fiancé vanished."

"I saw a portrait of an older fellow downstairs. Is that Viktor?"

Diana nodded. "Yes, that's him."

Tiffany was curious now. "Who was his fiancé?"

Alan cut in before Diana could say anything. "That's another thing. This fiancé of his doesn't have a name."

"I'm telling you, Viktor saw ghosts, and he fell in love with one." Diana said matter-of-factly.

Alan laughed. "That's crazy talk." He took a bite of his taco. "Let's finish our supper without bringing up ghosts."

Lucas looked over to Rose and said: "By the way, Rose, we have some people coming to fix the house tomorrow. They should be done within a week."

That pleased Rose. "Okay, sounds good."

After supper she headed back to the basement and put on more comfortable clothes. This time she looked around at everything, noticing things she hadn't earlier. A display case in one corner was filled with random knickknacks. There were things from China and India and even a ship in a bottle. On the very bottom sat an old box; the color had faded and the beautiful fabric that once decorated it was tearing away.

Curious, Rose opened the latch on the display case and reached in for the box. It weighed almost nothing and smelled like a musty old attic in an old person's home. Rose carefully opened the box and found a lock of blond hair tied with a black string.

She also noticed that the box's bottom could be lifted out. Under that she found a poorly drawn picture of a young woman. Rose guessed that the lock of hair had belonged to her.

Rose thought back to the dream she had about the man. Perhaps she was more prone to seeing things now that she had seen Elizabeth's ghost and had spent so much time at the mansion. Could Viktor Slater have a connection to it all? Rose would have to ask Edmond. She still had the photos on her phone from the museum and wanted to show him those, too. She stood up quickly and took a picture of Viktor Slater. There were still so many secrets left to unravel.

The week went by faster than Rose thought it would. Alan and Diana were just as full of adventure as Rose and offered many times to take her on short trips to show her around England's hidden treasures. And when it came time to head back to the house, Rose was a little disappointed, but she knew she would have other opportunities like this before leaving. Her first plan of action was to head to the mansion as soon as she returned, but there were too many things to do before she could leave her parents.

The windows in the house had been repaired and so had the leaky roof over her parents' bedroom. None of these cost them a penny as they did not own the home, nor did it cost Alan and Diana anything. It was caused by a natural disaster, and the town paid for it. New carpet had been laid in all the rooms that had water damage, and even Rose's bed was replaced.

Edmond's jacket was still there, and so was Elizabeth's dress. That was all Rose cared about— and that the diary was safely hidden away in her suitcase.

As Rose sat on her bed clutching Edmond's jacket, she wondered what it would be like to live forever.

Chapter Nine

The following day, as Rose made her way to the mansion, she was nearly skipping with glee. Her parents had left the house again, this time to meet up with some more old friends, so Rose did not have to worry about them asking where she was going. She knew they would be back late.

Edmond and Thackeray had become Rose's second family. They had put so much trust in each other that Rose had fallen for them. They were her friends, her treasure, and essentially her little secret.

Rose had decided to bring chocolate bars and soda pop on this outing, mainly to see their reactions. She bet that Thackeray would love both.

When Rose arrived, Thackeray was in the front yard gathering flowers into a small, weathered basket.

"Good morning, Thackeray," Rose said as she let herself in the front gate.

Thackeray smiled when he saw her. "Oh, Rose, good morning. I'm so glad to see you. I haven't seen you for a while. I hope everything is all right."

"Yeah, I'm okay," she replied. "There was some damage done to the house, so my parents and I stayed with some friends while it was being fixed."

Thackeray eyed Rose's bag. "What have you got in there?" he asked.

Rose put a finger to her lips. "That's a secret." She giggled. "Shall we go see what Edmond is up to?"

Thackeray brushed the dirt off his pants and smiled. "Yes, let's."

Edmond was in the library reading. He sat cross-legged and slouched, but when he saw Rose, he straightened himself up and put down his book. "Rose, what a surprise!" He stood up and greeted her with a soft kiss to the cheek. "I did not think I'd see you today."

"I'm sorry," she said with an apologetic smile. "I just told Thackeray that the house was wrecked, and my parents and I were forced to stay somewhere else until the damage was fixed. I came back as soon as I could." She reached inside her bag and pulled out a chocolate bar. "And I brought gifts."

Edmond gave the chocolate bar an odd look but took it anyway and read the label. "What is this?" he asked.

"That is a chocolate bar," Rose told him. "I brought one for each of us. And I have a few soda pops." She pulled one out.

Edmond cocked his head to the side. "Soda pop?"

Rose laughed. "You drink it." She cracked one open, allowing the hissing gases to escape, and took a sip. "It's grape flavor. Want to try it?"

Edmond hesitated. "One at a time."

Thackeray was quick to butt in. "Rose, may I have a taste of it?"

Rose handed him the drink. "You're not afraid of germs, are you?"

Thackeray shook his head. "No," he said with a chuckle and took a sip. "Wow! This is amazing. Edmond, you must have some." He pushed the drink into his friend's hand.

Now both Rose and Thackeray were looking at him.

"Well, go ahead, try it," Rose said as she handed Thackeray a chocolate bar.

Edmond took a sip of the drink first, his face twisting up a little. "No, thank you," he said, handing the soda back to Rose. "It's nice of you, but I don't think I can handle more of it." He then eyed the chocolate bar suspiciously and unwrapped it, first sniffing it before taking a bite.

Rose and Thackeray waited for his response.

"I approve of this." He smiled a little and handed it to Thackeray to try.

After they finished their snacks, Thackeray sat down at the piano and played.

Rose then remembered the photos she had taken at the museum. "Hey, Edmond," she said, pulling out her phone, "I have some things to show you."

Curious, Edmond asked, "Oh? What things?"

Rose was quick to find the photos on her phone and held the first one up for Edmond to see. "Does this woman look familiar to you?"

Edmond gave it a good look. "No, she doesn't. Where did you see it, may I ask?"

"At a museum in London. I thought she looked a little like Elizabeth, so I thought that maybe you would know something."

Edmond shook his head. "I'm afraid not."

Rose then swiped to the next picture. "What about this one? The painter's name was never mentioned. And you see this?" she said, zooming in on the piano in the photo. "It looks like the piano here."

Edmond studied it longer than the last, admiring it almost. "I haven't seen this painting in ages," he said.

Rose smiled. "So, you do know about it?"

Edmond nodded. "Of course I do. The boy in the painting is me."

Rose's jaw dropped, and Thackeray stopped playing.

"What?" Rose exclaimed.

"I thought it was destroyed in the fire," Edmond said, more to himself than to the others.

Rose could hardly believe it. "This is really you, Edmond?"

"I was only six in that painting." He rubbed his neck. "Thinking back on that moment brings that kink back in my neck."

"You look like a cute little prince," Rose said.

128

This time Edmond laughed. "I'm glad you like it so much."

"There are others who really like it, too, besides me," Rose added.

"Oh really." Edmond was curious now.

Rose nodded. "People were fascinated by it at the museum," she said. "Who was the painter?"

Edmond tried hard to remember. "I can't remember his name, but he was French."

Edmond and Rose suddenly realized Thackeray had stopped playing music.

"What's the matter, Thackeray?" Edmond asked.

Thackeray slipped off the seat and smoothed the wrinkles in his pants. "I've been contemplating on when we should go hunting. The fish haven't been biting, and the food from the garden is getting scarce." In all honesty, Thackery no longer wanted to talk about what was lost in the fire.

Edmond rubbed his chin. "You are right about this."

Rose set her bag to the side. "If you two go hunting, can I join you?"

"Are you sure?" Edmond asked, giving her a puzzled look. "Have you ever gone hunting before?"

Rose shook her head as if embarrassed. "No."

"Do girls hunt in this day and age?" Edmond asked.

"Yeah, some do," she replied with a shrug.

Edmond thought for a moment. "Are you sure you want to join us? I don't want you getting hurt."

"Let's have her give it a try, Edmond," Thackeray chimed in.

Edmond stood up and gave Rose a good look. "I guess what you're wearing will be fine. It's a good thing you're not in a dress."

"So, I can go?" Rose asked excitedly.

"You can go." Edmond told her.

Rose leaped and thrust a fist into the air. "Yay! This will be so fun, guys."

Thackeray laughed. "You're funny, Rose."

The trio walked into a part of the forest Rose had never been to. The trees and bushes denser, and the three were well hidden, although it also made it more difficult to get a clear shot.

Rose walked in between the two, with Edmond leading the way. He had a good eye for hunting and knew exactly where to look. Rose couldn't stop admiring his broad shoulders, thinking how much she would like to wrap her arms around him again. She wanted to play with his hair, too. His ponytail swaying in the wind was an unintentional tease.

Edmond stopped suddenly and signaled with his hand to be quiet.

A few yards away stood a buck, its antlers long and thick.

Edmond steadied himself as he raised his pistol; no one dared breathe. A shot fired, smoke rising from his pistol. He had struck the buck squarely in the head. An easy kill for him.

Thackeray took out his rope and quickly tied it around the buck's legs. He and Edmond grabbed both ends and started hauling it back toward the mansion.

"Can I help?" Rose asked.

Thackeray didn't mind the offer. "You can help me." He was up front, unable to drag the heavier bottom half.

"Okay, I can do that," she said.

When they reached the mansion, they dragged the carcass into the kitchen and lifted it up onto the cooking table. Thackeray quickly set out buckets on the floor.

"What are the buckets for?" Rose asked.

Edmond put on an apron and grabbed a long knife from the counter and wiped it clean. "You may want to step out for this," he warned her.

"Oh," said Rose. "You're going to skin and gut it, I see." She took in a deep breath. "I'll be fine. Go for it," she told him.

Edmond admired her bravery and swiftly pierced the buck to cut it in half. Thackeray pulled out the guts, his sleeves rolled up and his apron tied tight so no blood would stain his clothes.

The buckets were used for different parts of the animal. One was for the intestines, and the other was for its liver, lungs, and heart.

The sight and smell finally got to Rose, and she stepped outside for some fresh air. A part of her thought that she would be able to handle it. But in the end it was more the smell than the sight of blood that made her bail.

As she looked up into the sky, her eyes closed, she could hear a soft swoosh high above her. She opened her eyes to see a plane through the branches. Her heart fell into her stomach as she remembered she would be leaving England soon. How much longer did she have? A month? A few weeks? She had begun to lose track of time.

She cursed the plane and wished she could stay longer, even for just an extra day. Rose told herself she would do anything to stay. And then she started to cry uncontrollably and walked away from the mansion so Thackeray and Edmond wouldn't hear her sniffling.

A light rain began falling, but there was no threat of another storm.

Maybe a terrible storm will delay our flight, thought Rose. Maybe we will be able to stay a few more days or maybe even another week? Such thoughts repeatedly ran through her mind. Rose leaned against a tree and tried to calm herself before returning to the mansion, but suddenly a voice called out her name.

"Rose, where are you?" It was Edmond.

Rose hurriedly wiped the tears away, but her eyes were red from all of the rubbing and crying. "I'm over here, Edmond," she replied, stepping out from behind the tree.

"There you are. Thackeray and I are finished. Everything has been cleaned and is being cooked." He stopped for a moment. "Rose, are you crying?"

Rose laughed a little. "I was."

"Why?"

Rose waved him off; she was feeling embarrassed and didn't want to further the discussion. "It's fine, really."

Edmond grabbed her hands. "What's the matter, Rose?"

Her tears welled up again, and her face scrunched up at the thought of the inevitable. "I don't want to leave." She pulled her hands from Edmond's grasp and buried her face in her palms, sobbing. "I want to stay here with you and Thackeray."

Edmond could hardly make out what she was saying, she was crying hard. It upset him to see her this way. "Then don't. You can stay here as long as you like, Rose." He moved her hands away from her face and gently wiped her tears away. To stop her quivering lips, he kissed her, softly sucking on her lower lip. He pulled her into his arms and held her tight.

Rose pressed her face against his chest. "You and Thackeray are my best friends. I love you guys."

"And we love you, Rose." Edmond hushed her as she continued to weep.

Rose, still grasping his shirt, pushed herself away. "Summer is almost over, Edmond. When summer ends, I have to go back to America." She didn't want to say the words but knew she had to.

Edmond caressed her hair, trying to remember every part of her. That's right. Rose was on vacation. It wasn't as if she was going to stay here forever. Unless …

Edmond tried to free his mind of the very idea of Rose drinking the potion. It was possible, though. If they were desperate enough to be together, Edmond could make it happen.

"Do not worry about that now, my dear Rose," Edmond told her. "Come, let us go inside and wait for supper."

While Thackeray kept an eye on the meat roasting, Rose and Edmond rested in his room. Candles were lit, and the two of them lay on the rug, snuggled together. Edmond read her poetry from a French writer, and Rose was awestruck by how well he knew the language. She could listen to him speak in that foreign tongue for hours.

Finally, Edmond set the book down and said to Rose, "What will you do when you go back to America?"

Taken aback by his question, she said wistfully, "I don't know."

"You can always come back here," he said.

Rose looked away. "If I can ever make it back."

"What do you mean?" Edmond asked.

Rose struggled to find the right words. "I don't know if I'll ever have this opportunity again." Rose looked back at Edmond. She had a feeling those words might have hurt him. "I'm sorry."

"Why do you apologize?" Edmond wanted to know.

Rose took a deep breath. "Because you may never see me again after I leave, and I don't want to be just a memory for you."

Edmond put a finger to Rose's lips. "I know that the choice you make will be the right one. I want you to do what you think is best for you." He leaned in and kissed her.

It pained Edmond to say this. He wanted her to drink the potion and stay with him forever, but would she turn her back on everyone else she knew? Should he even try to persuade her?

And then she said it. "Tell me about the potion, Edmond."

He was surprised she brought it up. "What do you want to know about it?" he asked, knowing in his gut that he shouldn't encourage the topic.

"Well, for starters," Rose began, "did it take effect right away?"

Edmond shook his head. "No. It takes a reasonably fair amount of consumption to really work. Drinking it has a different effect on different people. For me, it made me feel weightless, and for Thackeray, it always made him feel tired."

"Could it kill anyone? You know, like backfire?"

Edmond thought about it. "I don't know. The potion was made to heal an illness, but I suppose it could be possible. I doubt it, though."

Rose was going to let the conversation end there, but then she remembered something. She pulled her phone out of her pocket and flipped through her photos again. "Does this man look familiar to you?" she asked, handing Edmond her phone.

It took him a moment, but Edmond remembered and handed Rose her phone back. "I suppose you want to know who he is?" She nodded, and Edmond sighed. "That's Viktor Slater. How did you come by this?"

"It was in the basement of the home I stayed in while the house was being worked on. Diana, the one who is friends with my parents, she is Viktor's great-great-great-great-granddaughter. Can you tell me about him, please?"

"Well, since you said 'please.' " Edmond prepared himself. "He was Elizabeth's betrothed."

Rose gave him a puzzled look. "But I thought she was your wife."

Edmond nodded. "She was, but she was promised to Viktor before me. There was nothing good about him, that Viktor Slater. He was power hungry and money grubbing."

"An asshole," Rose commented.

Edmond raised a brow at her. "Indeed. That bloody man made my life a living hell, and Elizabeth's, too."

Rose ran her fingers through his hair. "We don't have to talk about him, if you don't want to."

Edmond grabbed her hand and kissed it. "You already know me so well." He grinned at her.

Rose was quick to take his hand and slipped one of his fingers into her mouth.

Edmond dropped his mouth, stunned.

When Rose saw the look on his face she stopped. "You don't like that?"

Edmond swallowed hard. "Quite the opposite,"

"Do you want me to do it again?" she asked.

Edmond fumbled with his words. "I don't think that's a good idea, Rose."

She smiled mischievously. "Why?" and slipped his finger back into her mouth before he could protest further.

Edmond made his move and rolled on top of Rose. He allowed both his hands to roam free on her body, and she didn't resist. The sensation that came over him was something he hadn't felt in years, and he succumbed to it.

"Rose, you have to tell me to stop," he begged, afraid of what he might do.

"No," she told him.

Edmond left trails of sweet kisses on her neck before lifting her shirt half way and caressing her belly with his lips. This made Rose giggle. To give himself an opportunity to compose his hunger, Edmond took off his shirt and tossed it to the side.

Rose reached up with greedy hands and rubbed his chest selfishly before searching for something else. Her fingertips stopped at the top of his pants and tugged at them, wanting them off so she could see what he hid underneath. Rose could see the bulge, and the size of him excited her. "Edmond," she whispered breathlessly.

Rose had teased him plenty of times before this, and now he had his opportunity to get back at her. He made her wait and took off her shirt, surprised to see what she wore underneath.

"What is this?" Edmond asked.

It then occurred to Rose that Edmond had never seen a bra. "This is a bra. Girls wear these to keep their breasts covered…like a corset."

Just as she was about to help him take off her bra, a soft knock sounded at the door, and they stopped.

"Supper is done, you two. It turned out great." It was Thackeray. "Hello?" His hand reached for the knob, but it just wiggled because the door was locked. "I'll be in the dining room setting everything up."

Edmond's face flushed red as the swelling in his pants subsided. He pulled himself from Rose and picked up his shirt. "We should join Thackeray before he starts to worry."

Rose wanted to continue, but she knew Edmond was right and reluctantly slipped on her shirt. She walked to the door and stopped when Edmond did not follow. "Are you coming?"

Edmond waited a few seconds before answering her. "Yes, I'll be down in a minute. Go ahead of me. I'll meet up with you two," he told her with his back to her.

One side of the dining table was covered with food. The hind of the buck they had slain lay thinly sliced on a silver platter. Other parts of it were used in a soup, while the liver and lungs were placed on a separate plate. Warm bread and sweet rolls and a bowl of mixed berries completed the meal.

Thackeray had expertly prepared the plates and poured each of them a glass of wine. He then lit every candle in the room to make up for the fading outside light.

"This looks and smells amazing, Thackeray," Rose said as she walked into the dining room. "I don't know where to begin." She took a seat and almost drooled at the sight of the delicious spread.

Thackeray smiled and took a seat. "I've had a long time to perfect my cooking skills." He grabbed a sweet roll and chowed down.

Edmond came striding through the doors, his hair neatly combed and his rosy cheeks back to their natural color. "Starting without me?" he teased and took a seat across from Rose and started eating.

There was joyful talk of the day as they ate, but Rose couldn't help but gaze at Edmond. She knew he could hardly look at her without thinking about what they nearly surrendered themselves to. Her fits of giggles started off small and grew into a belly laugh.

"What's the matter with her?" Thackeray asked, puzzled by her bubbly responses.

Edmond had a good idea, but he wasn't going to say anything. "Maybe it's something you put in the food."

Thackeray rolled his eyes, a grin appearing on his face.

When Rose stopped laughing, she apologized and went back to eating, and the remainder of their meal was spent in happy conversation.

Afterward, they retired to the music room. Thackeray played the piano softly, with Rose at his side. Edmond lay on the sofa staring at the ceiling and listening. No words needed to be spoken to know how each of them was feeling.

Music echoed throughout the mansion, its soft, harmonious tones wafting through the hallways. Each was a tiny moment that would last only for seconds before becoming a memory of a time that once was. How long would these stone walls hold in the light and sounds of music and laughter?

How long before all the windows finally broke, only to be boarded up? The mansion wept happily. Her years of growing restless were coming to an end, and acceptance became tolerable.

At sundown Edmond walked Rose back to the house. He wanted to make sure she made it back safely, plus it was an excuse to spend more time with her.

"There is something I must tell you before we part ways," Edmond said, stopping in his tracks.

Rose looked up into his face as the light of the moon shined upon them through the leaves. "You can tell me anything."

"It's about Viktor."

Rose nodded, allowing him to continue.

"He came looking for us years after the massacre. Why he waited so long, I know not the reason. Perhaps he truly loved Elizabeth?"

Rose was a bit shocked. "He found you?"

Edmond nodded feebly. "No one ever thought he would show his face, so when he did, we had no time to run. He saw Elizabeth first. And when he finally saw me, he became angry and called me every nasty name he possibly could. I quickly grew fed up with his attitude and swung at him, knocking him to the floor." He paused for a second.

"It was Elizabeth who stepped between us, but Viktor acted in haste and pushed Elizabeth to the side and came at me with a knife." Edmond touched his stomach. "He stabbed me, but of course my wound quickly healed, and the blood stopped coming. When he saw this, he threatened to tell everyone, but I couldn't let him do that, and he was forcing my hand to commit an act of murder. I didn't want to kill him, but he was pushing me to my breaking point."

Rose put a hand to her mouth. "What happened after that?"

Edmond continued. "Elizabeth stopped and told me that we had to

138

give him a chance and to speak to him properly. By this time Viktor was already out the door, and Elizabeth went after him. I would have followed immediately, but I was shaking with anger and fear and stood there trying to compose myself. By the time I ran after them, they were far ahead of me."

"Where was Thackeray when all of this was happening?" asked Rose.

"Thackeray was the smart one," Edmond said. "He stayed out of it for as long as he could. We all knew he would have been no match for Viktor in physical strength, but he had another means of dealing with our precarious situation."

Rose shot him a cross look. "Edmond, what did Thackeray do?"

Edmond almost wished he had not said anything, but telling Rose was the right thing to do. If a thread of hope lingered and Rose stayed, she had to know these things. "Thackeray shot him. I remember the sound echoing through the trees and Elizabeth's cry for him to stop, but it was too late, and I watched as she comforted Viktor in his final moments. I was almost jealous of him." Edmond stopped, trying to steady his emotions. "I will never forget the sight of Thackeray as he stepped out from the bushes. His face was filled with guilt and torment. Don't you see, Rose, it should have been me who killed him, not poor Thackeray.

"The grave holds every soul that ever died on this land, Viktor included," Edmond added. "You must understand and accept this if you are to stay here with us." He kissed her. "Goodnight, Rose."

Rose kissed him back and said goodbye when they got within sight of the house. Edmond waited to make sure she safely got inside before leaving.

As Rose made her way in through the back door, she heard her parents. A sinking feeling filled her gut as she realized that they must have noticed she was gone. She made her way to the living room and from the doorway could see they were watching television and talking with friends.

"Oh, Rose, hi! Glad you could join us," Tiffany said when she finally noticed her daughter. "Are we too loud?"

Rose tried not to look confused. "No, you didn't bother me. When did you guys get back?"

Lucas looked at her strangely. "You mean you didn't hear us come in? We got back just a few minutes ago and just ordered pizza. Were you sleeping?"

Rose nodded. "Yeah, and I'm not very hungry."

"But you love pizza," said Tiffany. "Are you sure you don't have room for one slice?"

Rose was still full from eating the buck and declined her mother's offer. "No, you guys enjoy it for me. I'll be upstairs. Goodnight, you two."

Rose waved to their friends before retreated to her bedroom and locking the door. She sighed as she opened the window and gazed out at the forest. Her face turned pink as she fantasized about her and Edmond's passionate moment. She wished to return to that ephemeral memory, longing for it to last forever.

The voices of the others could be heard from downstairs as Rose contemplated her decision. It would be final and could not be made recklessly. The idea of living forever with Edmond and Thackeray flattered her, but she had her family to think about as well.

Chapter Ten

It was morning as Rose sat near a window in a small coffee shop. She had woken up early that day and decided to get breakfast and coffee with her parents or, in this case, tea.

It hadn't rained in the last couple of days, so the air was warmer, and the sun was no longer hiding behind clouds.

Rose could hear her parents talking, but her attention was on what was going on outside.

"How about it, Rose?" her mother asked.

Rose redirected her gaze to her mother. "Hmm?"

"Your dad and I were thinking about going to see another castle before we have to leave," said Tiffany.

"We were thinking that maybe we could visit one further away, maybe see a bit more of the countryside," Lucas added.

Rose had seen a few castles already, but she was always up to see more. "Yeah, I'd love to go." She took a sip of her green tea.

Tiffany could sense her daughter was holding back. "Is everything okay, sweetie?" she asked.

Rose wasn't sure what her mother was getting at. "Yeah, I'm fine. It's just...we'll be leaving soon."

"We can always come back to England someday," Lucas told her. "It's not like we won't have other opportunities like this."

What Lucas said stung. What if Rose didn't have another opportunity to come back? What if she never saw Thackeray and Edmond again?

"I know," Rose said.

Suddenly, she jumped at the sound of a crash. Outside the window a man riding a bike had been struck by a car. People ran to his aid while others stood around in shock. Rose watched intently as the cyclist was cared for by strangers, and finally the man who had hit him got out of his car. He was obviously upset and holding his head as if trying not to cry.

The wail of sirens could be heard as an ambulance pulled up, but the man on the bike had walked away with just a few scratches and a sprained arm. Rose was so focused on what was going on outside that she hadn't noticed her food being placed down in front of her.

"Rose, your food," Lucas said.

"Oh, yeah," she said, picking up a knife and cutting her cinnamon bun in half.

When they finished breakfast, Rose and her parents started out on their road trip. They drove three hours, stopping occasionally to take pictures or to get gas. They were headed northwest to see the castle of Dartmouth; there was an old church beside it and a lookout tower nearby. The town of Dartmouth sat at the edge of the sea, and with the tide at rest Rose was able to enjoy the beach. She kept busy walking the shoreline and eating ice cream while lost in thought. It was clear that she would not be seeing Edmond or Thackeray today, but that was okay with her.

The sky was clear and the sea breeze cool. How long had these waves been rolling back and forth? A year? A decade? A century? Perhaps since the beginning of time? Rose thought what it would be like to go on forever, just like these waves. Would she stay as she was at this very moment—young and beautiful? She could do it, drink the potion. Edmond could easily make it for her. She could drink it before leaving and then return and revert to her youthful self. But what if she did drink it and decide not to go back; would she turn into dust just as Elizabeth did after reaching a certain age? There wasn't much time left for her to think about it. A choice had to be made.

142

On the way back to the house, Rose looked at her parents from the back seat. What would happen if she suddenly vanished? Her parents probably would never stop looking for her. The real question, though, was: would she be able to do it? She would have to fake her death in order to stay.

The endless possibilities of what could happen filled Rose's mind. She couldn't stop thinking about it, the thoughts tormenting her. Finally, she sighed, rolled down the window, and let the wind blow away some of the stress.

By the time they arrived back at the house, it was late and Rose was exhausted. She sat at the vanity table brushing her hair in front of the mirror. Each time she looked at her reflection, she was a bit older. Rose took the brush and examined the hairs that were caught in the bristles. Soon those strands of hair would be gray and her skin would start to sag with age. She just hoped the light would never fade from her eyes.

What kind of life would she lead if she were to return to America? Maybe she would marry and have children. Or maybe she would live a life of solitude.

Rose walked over to her bed and saw Elizabeth's diary on the nightstand. "I don't know what to do," she said disconsolately as she lay in bed. She grabbed the diary. "I need an answer," she whispered to herself and began to read. Rose had put off reading the diary long enough, worried about what she might learn. There was no turning back now.

1779, 5th of August,

Dear Diary,

Edmond was acting like his usual self today: rude and annoying. You see, as I was enjoying my cup of tea and plate of cookies, Edmond squirted tea at his tutor. Can you believe that, my own friend spitting tea at a grown man? How childish of him. Then again, we are not yet adults, so I guess it's safe to assume that we are still children, but still.

I was also surprised to see that his tutor returned his action in kind. Edmond was not happy to have received the same treatment. It serves him right, though, I say. My dear, if Edmond were to read this, he would get so upset with me, although Edmond has never been angry with me. He has always treated me well. I must admit, though, when this happened I laughed, and this Edmond did not like. He put his head down in shame and was embarrassed.

Luckily, I found him later in the forest. He was clearly upset, as he was throwing rocks and sticks. I had wanted to apologize to him for laughing, but I found myself asking him if he was still mad about what happened with his tutor. When I said this, I knew I had surprised him. He turned around quickly with a rock in his hand, ready to throw it. I told him he wouldn't dare, and if he did he would really have something to worry about.

Edmond lowered his hand, still looking embarrassed. He told me he wasn't going to throw it, that he was just upset.

I walked up to him and took the rock from his hand and tossed it to the ground. I asked him why, because he was the one who started it.

Edmond became angry, but he quickly calmed himself, as he always did when I was around. He told me that it was his home that no one had the right to challenge his authority. And then he went on about having him dismissed!

I couldn't help but scoff at him. He was acting so dumb, and I told him this. He was being childish. "You're almost eighteen." I told him.

Edmond laughed. He said that what I said was funny, seeing how I'm barely twelve years old.

I stomped on his foot to let him know I was serious. "And I act more grown up than you." I couldn't help but say it.

I could tell he wanted to yell at me, try to put me in my place. But my place was far from where he was standing, and I think he knew this, for he suddenly calmed himself with a deep sigh. And finally, he said he would go apologize to Mr. Adams.

Before Edmond could walk away from me I said to him that I came here to apologize, but I could see that he didn't need an apology from a child.

Edmond rolled his eyes at me but thanked me nonetheless.

I smiled at him. "How would you ever manage without me?" I took his hand and walked back to the mansion, and I made sure that he really did apologize to his tutor.

Sometimes I wonder if Edmond will only ever see me as a little girl.

The writing was beginning to fade, so Rose skipped a few pages until she found another entry that was visible enough to read.

1781, 1st of October,

Dear Diary,

My eyes burn from crying so much that I can hardly keep them open to write. Father and mother came to me this morning after breakfast and told me that they have found a suitable husband for me. I am only thirteen! They say I am to marry a man named Viktor Slater. He is three times my age. Father and mother say that I will be spending every Tuesday and Friday with him until I turn seventeen, and then I am to marry him. I don't want to get to know him.

No matter how much I try to reason with my parents, they will not listen to me. They think they know what is best for me, but I am frightened of Mr. Slater.

Even as I try to write now, I am trying to hold back my tears. I don't want to spoil this diary with my tears. I am hurt and confused and angry.

My parents do not understand. All they care about is how much money Mr. Slater is worth. I'd rather live poor for the rest of my days and be married to a man I love than rich and jailed into a marriage I dread.

What should I say to Edmond when I see him next? Of all the men in the world my parents could have chosen, they chose Viktor Slater. Did they even consider Edmond? I must ask them this. I have to try, or perhaps I'm not suitable enough for him. Maybe my parents did ask him and he said no.

I'm so scared.

1781, 20th of December,

Dear Diary,

I told Edmond about the engagement. I could hardly look at him when I did. We stood in silence in the music room for a long time before he said anything. He looked irritated, but most of all he looked disappointed.

He told me that I was always welcome here and kissed my cheek before walking away.

He confuses me with these kind and simple gestures toward me. Does he care about me romantically, or is this friendship all we have? Our friendship means more to me than I think he realizes. Maybe I should just come out and confess my feelings for him?

What astonished me next was that he invited Mr. Slater to his home. He had arrived after my parents and I had. We were all get together for some tea, and I detested the very idea. And as I watched Edmond speak with Viktor, I understood what he was doing. Edmond was studying him to see if he was fit enough, and if Viktor ever caught on to this, he made no sign to say otherwise.

I wish my parents would see that Edmond is a better match for me. We have grown up together, and we know much about one another: what pleases us, what displeases us, our hopes, and our fears. Why did it have to be Mr. Slater?

1782, 6th of February,

Dear diary,

Edmond and Viktor got into a fight today. It was right after a game of swordplay. Edmond lost, and then he lost his temper. He shouted at Viktor, telling him that his very presence made him sick.

Viktor's response to this was, "I beg your pardon?" He didn't seem offended at all, but I could sense that he liked the challenge.

Edmond warned him not to play dumb with him, and I watched as he balled his fists and his face turned shades of red.

My mother tried escorting me out of the room, but I refused to go. I wanted to watch their fight. Immediately after that my father and a few male servants stepped between them, but the tension was still there and my father immediately told him to calm down.

Of course, Edmond would not. The confidence in his voice filled me with hope. Finally, Edmond's eyes softened as he looked over at me. He told my parents that Viktor was not a suitable husband, that he is a fake and beyond repair. He took a breath and said, "I will not let her become damaged goods." Those words rang in my ears as he said this to my father and shot a glare at Viktor.

My father called for silence in the room. He explained that I would marry Viktor because he and my mother say so. And then he continued to insult Edmond by saying just because he owns a mansion and runs it with full authority doesn't mean he knows everything. "And keep your bloody opinions to yourself." He finished.

My father took my hand and pulled me along, and when I looked back, I saw Viktor whisper something to Edmond and his face turned white. What occurred next happened so fast that I couldn't stop it. Edmond hit Viktor so hard that he fell to the floor.

Everyone in the room was so appalled that they could do nothing but stare. And as Viktor picked himself up and smoothed his hair, he spat blood at Edmond's feet. I thought that would be the extent of Viktor's comeback, but I was wrong. Viktor lunged at Edmond and brought him to the floor. It was only after that did the servants manage to rip the two apart.

When everything quieted, and Viktor had left, I searched for Edmond whilst our carriage was being readied and found him in the library looking helplessly out the window.

I called out to him softly, but he didn't seem to hear me, so I called out to him again and placed a hand on his shoulder. He shrugged me away and refused to look at me. I called out to him again and asked if he was all right. I heard a sniffle and by my surprise Edmond was crying. I could hardly believe it. Edmond Valcain crying?

This time I forced him to look at me. His face was bruising where Viktor had hit him, and his eyes were puffy. He asked me if I was really going to marry Viktor.

"That man." He said. There was something in his voice that made it sound like the greatest insult.

I sighed, not sure what to say to him. Finally, I told him that was the way things had to be. I regretted saying that as soon as it came out of my mouth.

Edmond rolled his eyes. He told me that Viktor doesn't love me, that he only wants to marry me because my parents will make him richer. He also said that Viktor doesn't care what kind of qualities I have. As long as he has a pretty wife and money in his pocket he doesn't care.

This surprised me. "You think I'm beautiful?"

Edmond dodged my question. "What's wrong with *me*?" He said that he had only ever been kind to me and my parents. This is true. After today my parents never had a reason to hate him.

"I don't know, Edmond."

Edmond huffed, saying that it was stupid and asking why I have to marry that pig.

"Because…"

Edmond was getting upset again, saying it was because my parents demanded it. He wasn't wrong.

"I suppose so." I looked down at my feet, ashamed for not being able to say more to him. And then, to my surprise, Edmond reached out to me and cupped my face in his hands. His hands were warm and smooth, not rough like I thought they would be.

"Marry me, Elizabeth." His words shocked me more than his sudden embrace. He told me that I should marry him when I turn seventeen and forget all about Viktor and what my parents say. He told me that if I married him I would never have to worry about my parents telling me what to do ever again.

I pulled away from Edmond. I couldn't possibly go against my parent's wishes, and I told him this.

Edmond wasn't happy to hear this. "You're promised to a lie, Elizabeth." I could tell he wanted to say more to me by the strain in his eyes, and then he said it: "I love you, Elizabeth. I have for a very long time."

I couldn't hold myself back any longer and whispered yes to him. I can still feel the sweet little kisses he gave me. It was hard for me to leave him, but I know I will see him again.

Rose set the diary down after that entry and rubbed her weary eyes. It was late, and there was much to think about.

Thackeray awoke early that same morning. He plopped his head back on his pillow as the sun was just starting to say hello and wondered why he had awaken so early. No matter how much he tried to fall back to sleep, something had disturbed him. He could hear the faint sounds of a piano, but who could it possibly be if Rose wasn't there? As tired as he was, Thackeray pulled himself out of bed and followed the sound of the music.

As he walked into the music room, he was startled to see Rose. He tiptoed carefully so as not to disrupt her, as she played so wonderfully. She looked beautiful in her summer dress, with her pretty auburn hair lying in perfect waves down her back.

It was only after she finished her piece did Thackeray make himself known.

"Good morning, Rose," he said, sitting down beside her. "What brings you here so early?"

Rose sighed. "I couldn't sleep."

Thackeray could see the anguish in her blue eyes. "What is the matter, Rose?"

"My time here is almost done." She admitted to this sadly, her hands shaking as they hovered over the keys.

Thackeray held her hands to calm her. "What do you mean?"

"I have to go back to America soon."

Thackeray wasn't sure what to say. He had grown so used to seeing Rose that he couldn't imagine what it would be like never to see her again. "You can always stay, Rose," he said tenderly. "Edmond and I would love to have you always."

Rose sniffled and wiped away a tear. "Thank you, Thackeray." She turned to him. "Don't tell Edmond this."

"Why?"

"I don't want him getting any ideas."

Thackeray chuckled at this. "I'm afraid Edmond is always getting ideas. It's hard to tell what he will do next."

Rose pulled her hands away from his and placed them on her lap. "To be perfectly honest, I don't know what I will do when the time comes for me to leave. At times I think I do, that I can stay and leave behind everything and start somewhere anew, and then I tell myself that that's impossible."

Thackeray looked to Rose, wishing she didn't feel so trapped. "You can always come back, Rose. Edmond and I will always be here for you." He started to play the piano. "Whatever choice you make, Rose, I will accept. If you want to stay, then I will support you. And if you decide to leave, then I will still support you. What I care about is your happiness."

Thackeray and Rose soon headed to the kitchen to prepare breakfast. They would make pancakes and pick out their favorite berries.

While the pancakes were cooking, Thackeray got started on making tea. He made his favorite green tea and let it steep while they turned their attention back to the pancakes.

Edmond came in just as breakfast was ready but stopped short in the doorway when he saw Rose.

"Rose!" Edmond said with surprise, his tired voice cracking. "What are you doing here so early?"

Rose finished piling the pancakes on a large platter and smiled at Edmond. "Is there something wrong for me to want to come and see you guys early?"

"Of course not," Edmond stammered.

"Good," Rose replied, handing him the platter. "Take this to the dining room, please."

Once the table was set, the trio sat down and enjoyed their meal in silence. No words needed to be exchanged to know how much they appreciated each other's company.

Chapter Eleven

Rose pushed the sheets off her as she lay in bed, too hot to get up. Her alarm clock had gone off for the sixth time, but even then she was too tired to shut it off. The last couple of days had been scorching hot, and the air conditioner could not keep up.

Finally, Rose sat up. Her body was sticky and her hair frizzy, and she smelled like the ocean. Rose and her parents had gone to the beach the day before and returned home so late that she didn't have the energy to wash up.

As her feet dangled off the edge of the bed, she stretched and looked across the room. Edmond's jacket was hanging in a corner, not far from Elizabeth's dress. Rose sighed, thinking back to the days when she received the jacket and the dress. She grabbed the jacket and pulled it close to her face. After all this time it still smelled like Edmond. If she left, would this be the only thing she'd have to remember him by? Rose tried not to think about that. More important now was for her to clean up, so she set down the jacket and prepared a bath.

When the temperature was just right, Rose stepped in, welcoming the feel of the cool water on her skin. It was the perfect antidote for a hot day. She let herself soak for a long while, sinking deep into the water. Her hair floated up like seaweed, and all sounds except the beating of her heart were muffled.

Rose closed her eyes and occasionally exhaled bubbles of air to allow herself to stay submerged longer. When she opened her eyes, a blurry, wavy figure loomed over her.

Startled, Rose shot up and gasped for air, almost choking. She grabbed the hand towel hanging over the edge of the tub and dried her face.

When she looked about the room, the figure was gone.

"Elizabeth," Rose said quietly. She felt silly for talking to herself, or was she?

Once Rose finished her bath, she quickly dressed and headed downstairs to find a note that her parents had left for her. They explained that they were going to visit with Alan and Diana and possibly stay the night. Alan and Diana's phone number was scribbled across the bottom of the note. Rose wouldn't need to call them, though, so she made her way to the mansion.

The sound of the rusty gates creaking as they opened no longer startled her. In fact, she was beginning to enjoy the sound.

Rose let herself in and called out to Edmond and Thackeray, but there was no response. She checked every room she thought they might be in, and even some she had never stepped foot in, but Edmond and Thackeray were nowhere to be found. It then occurred to her that they might be outside, seeing how it was stuffy inside the mansion even with a few windows open.

The back yard seemed as quiet as ever as Rose continued to look for the two. She checked the garden and the small shed covered in vines and weeds. Still, there was no sign of them.

Rose headed for the forest and eventually happened across the stream, where she found Thackeray. His shirt and shoes were off and his pant legs were rolled up as he stood in the water. He was splashing about, scaring the fish away, his fishing gear nowhere to be seen.

"Thackeray!" Rose called out to him and ran to meet him at the water's edge.

Thackeray was surprised and pleased to see her. "Hello, Rose. You look very beautiful today."

Rose smiled. "Oh, thank you, Thackeray." She slipped off her sandals and dipped her feet into the water.

Thackeray joined her and they sat in silence for a moment, "Edmond loves you, you know," he said earnestly.

Rose's heart skipped a beat. "I know he does," replying as if admitting it was a bad thing.

"Do you love him, Rose?"

Rose was taken aback by his words. "Of course I do," she answered after a pause.

And then Thackeray spoke slowly, as though he was walking on a thin line. "Do you love him enough to stay?"

Rose was feeling overwhelmed again. "What are you trying to say, Thackeray?"

Thackeray played with a rock by his feet. "I just want Edmond to be happy." He paused. "I want both of you to be happy."

No matter what choice Rose would end up making, she knew someone was going to get hurt. Either way, she would end up losing someone, whether it be her parents or Edmond and Thackeray.

"I want that, too, Thackeray," Rose said.

Thackeray's next words surprised Rose even more. "Do you love me?"

Rose placed an arm around him and said, "I do love you, Thackeray."

Thackeray permitted himself to be embraced. He hadn't felt this kind of touch since Elizabeth. He missed her now more than ever.

There were two people Thackeray had a hard time remembering—his parents—and he felt ashamed for it. The last memory he had of his father was watching him walk out the door. At first Thackeray's innocent mind thought he was going out to buy medicine for his sick mother, but he never returned, and the whereabouts of his father remained a mystery. He was left with just his sickly mother and the housemaid, but even the housemaid stopped coming, and he was left alone at the tender age of five with his ill mother.

When his mother passed, Thackeray was all alone, and he sat quietly next to her body. People eventually came to collect money, but when they saw that only poor Thackeray was there, they kicked him out of his home and dumped his mother's body into a nameless grave. That was when he was forced out onto the streets and would remain there for a long time. He slept in alleyways and in abandoned houses until someone bigger came along and forced him out.

Eventually, most of his clothes were taken from him, and he grew weak after having food stolen from him. He was always the little guy and constantly being pushed around. And then he met Edmond. Thackeray could remember that night well. His feet were blistered and frostbitten, and with one last desperate attempt for salvation, Thackeray weakly tugged on Edmond's coat.

Edmond stared down at him, his hazel eyes glistening in the pale moonlight, then picked him up and carried him to his carriage.

Thackeray easily remembered all this. Edmond looked almost like a god to him, a beautiful angel.

"What is your name, boy?" asked Edmond, his voice soothing.

Despite his teeth chattering from the cold, Thackeray managed to say his name.

That night he was pulled away from his destitute life and brought to what seemed at first like heaven. He slept until noon on feather-filled pillows and cotton-filled beds, instead of straw, and there was no one to take those comforts away from him.

The mansion was where Thackeray learned to read and write and play musical instruments. It was his safe place.

"Thackeray." Rose's voice snapped him back to the present. "Are you okay?"

"Yes, I'm fine," he answered quickly.

Rose thought for a moment. "Do you know where I could find Edmond?"

Thackeray paused before answering. "He's at the grave. You remember where that is?"

Rose nodded. "I do. Is he all right?"

"You will see when you get there. It is not my place to say." It was all he was going to tell her. "If you want to see Edmond, you better go now before he wanders off somewhere else."

"What will you do?"

Thackeray sighed. "Same as I always do: remain here."

Rose stood up hesitantly, afraid to leave Thackeray by himself. She patted him softly on the shoulder before leaving.

As Thackeray said, Edmond was in the graveyard. Rose was about to approach him but stopped short. He was on his knees with his head bowed, and his shoulders were shaking.

"Edmond?" Rose called out softly.

Edmond raised his head and wiped his sleeve across his face. "You shouldn't be here."

"Did I do something wrong?" Rose asked.

Edmond, with his back still turned, just shook his head. "No, but I need to be left alone right now."

Rose was about to turn away but stopped when she noticed Edmond clutching something. It was clothing, but it looked too small to belong to even a child.

Rose brought a hand to her mouth. "Your son," she said, looking past Edmond, and spotting a gravestone marked Benjamin Valcain. "I'm

156

sorry, Edmond."

Rose knelt beside him and looked at his tear-stained face. "Edmond, I need to speak with you. It's very important."

Edmond wiped away the remainder of his tears and stood up. "What is it that you wish to speak to me about?"

Many things were running through her mind, but there was only thing that absolutely needed saying. "I'm leaving in a week to go back to America."

Edmond couldn't conceal the hurt in his eyes. "So soon?" he asked.

"I have to go back, Edmond."

Edmond grabbed her hands. "No, you don't."

Rose sighed. "How do you expect me to stay?"

Edmond cleared his throat. "I have a well-thought-out plan. I'm no stranger to keeping things hidden." He glanced at the grave. "As you can see..."

"What are you trying to say, Edmond?" Rose was afraid to learn what his idea was.

"I can easily make it look as if you were killed by an animal. It would take just a small amount of your blood, and then I could send whoever is looking for you in the opposite direction. They would never find you. And when the time is right, you can drink the potion."

Rose caressed his cheek softly. "You know I can't do that."

Edmond squeezed her hands gently. "I don't want to live forever if it's not with you. Please, don't walk out of my life."

Rose fought back tears. "You make this so difficult."

"Are you scared?" Edmond suddenly asked. "Scared about living forever?"

Rose bit her lower lip, thinking aloud. "I'm just uncertain, that's all."

Edmond looked her straight in the eyes. "If you leave, you'll grow up…grow old. We may never see each other again. Do you want that?"

Rose nodded just once. "Yes, I know very well what could happen." She pulled her hand away. "Don't make this harder for me."

Edmond stood up straighter, regaining his composure. "I won't need to," he said.

"Edmond," Rose said, "I just want the next week to go by without any more about me leaving. Let's spend the rest of our time together like we always have. Can you do that for me…for us?"

Edmond nodded thoughtfully. "Of course, Rose. Anything for you."

Rose smiled, glad that he would drop the subject. "Good, because my parents will be gone until tomorrow, so I'm staying the night, okay?"

The mansion was filled with laughter that evening. The three prepared an exquisite meal of wild berries, meat pie, and soup with homemade bread and three different bottles of wine. Edmond was especially proud of the wine, which he had made and had stored in the cellar for the last five years.

As Rose had requested, there was no talk about her leaving, only room for playful gestures and innocent conversation. It was exactly what Rose wanted. She wanted to leave England with a good memory.

When night fell and candles were lit, Thackeray was struggling to stay awake. Eventually, Edmond carried him to his bed, with Rose following close behind. Once they tucked him in, they walked back to Edmond's room to enjoy the rest of their evening.

Edmond read poetry to Rose again, only this time in Spanish. She would sigh from time to time as she listened to tales of Spain and its lovers. She adored every one of them.

Suddenly, Rose took the book from Edmond and set it down, cuddling next to him. "Edmond, there is something I want you to do for me."

Edmond rested his head on top of hers. "Whatever you want, Rose."

Rose took a big breath. "The house where I am staying, there are paintings in the attic, and some of them are of Elizabeth. I'm pretty sure anyway. Did you ever paint her?"

Edmond took a moment to respond. "I did."

Rose sat up and looked at Edmond. "I want you to paint me, too."

Edmond grew nervous. "Before you leave we shall make it happen," he promised.

Rose shook her head. "No, tonight."

Edmond cocked his head to one side. "But, Rose, all my paint is dry. I haven't painted for many years." Edmond saw a look of disappointment spread across her face. "I think I may have some chalk." Edmond walked over to the side of his bed and began rummaging beneath it. He finally found what looked like a long, thin box covered in a white sheet. As Edmond brought it out and set it up in the middle of the room, he pulled off the sheet, exposing a blank canvas.

Rose stood up and next to Edmond. "It doesn't feel as if I've been here for three months." She rested her head on his shoulder. "It feels so much shorter."

Edmond smiled. "I had lost track of time and what it stood for until you came here. Now it seems like I will never have enough of it, no matter how long I live." Edmond turned toward Rose and brought her face to look at him. "I want to capture you in this moment." He caressed her hair lovingly and kissed her forehead.

Edmond pulled up a chair and arranged the candles so when he drew Rose, the light would be where he wanted it.

"Wait," she said and started to undress. She set her clothes down carefully and hesitated when she reached to unlatch her bra.

Edmond stood there in shock, unable to move or say anything, until he blurted out, "There is no need for that."

Rose stopped short, her hands still holding onto the back of her bra. "It is fine, Edmond. You want to remember me, right?"

"You are beautiful just how you are," he told her.

Rose smiled sweetly. "Too late," and she unhooked her bra, slid the straps off her shoulders, and let it drop to the floor. Rose removed every piece of clothing save for her underwear and sat back in the chair. "You can draw me now."

Edmond swallowed hard and began to draw. He was slow at first, trying to remember how he used to use the easel and also to regain his composure after seeing Rose.

The flickering candlelight brought warm shadows across Rose's body as she sat there patiently. The only sounds were those of Edmond's chalk sliding across the easel.

When he finished, his hands were smudged with chalk, and he brushed them across his pants to try to it get it off.

"Would you like to see?"

When Rose nodded, Edmond carefully turned the easel around. "My work is sloppy, so I hope you don't mind how it turned out."

There was no reason to apologize, though. Edmond's talents were astounding.

Rose gasped softly. "Is that what I really look like?"

Edmond was unsure of what she meant by that. "You don't like it?"

Rose laughed. "No, I love it!"

Edmond was shocked and also thrilled. "I'm very happy you like it so much." He brushed his fingers across Rose's naked back. "This is how I see you, Rose."

Rose admired the drawing a moment longer before wrapping her arms around Edmond and forcing herself on him. She gave him a deep kiss, refusing to let go.

"Is this what you want?" Edmond asked. "I don't want you to end up regretting this moment."

Rose started to unbutton his shirt. "There is nothing to regret," she said as she pulled his shirt off and pressed her body against his.

Edmond carried Rose to the bed and set her down gently. He held her close as they lay together, giving each other tender kisses. He moved his hands slowly over her body and slipped off her underpants. He then removed the rest of his clothes.

"Is this what you really want?" he asked again.

Rose blushed, nodding, and together they became one.

As the sun rose, Rose awoke to the sound of a bird singing outside the window. She rolled over to find Edmond still asleep and reached to touch his face but stopped. She didn't want to wake him.

Rose lay there for some time, thinking about what she should do. Soon she sat up and removed the covers, retrieved her clothes from the floor, and dressed. She checked the time on her phone and quietly cursed. It wasn't late, but she wanted to give herself enough time to get back to the house before he parents returned. She didn't know when they would get back.

Rose didn't want to leave Edmond without saying goodbye, but she knew she would have at least one more day with him. She closed the bedroom door as quietly as she could and tiptoed down the hallway.

"You're not staying for breakfast?" a small voice called out to her.

Rose stopped at the front doors and looked back to see Thackeray. "I want to get back before my parents do. Don't worry; I'll be back."

"Do you promise?"

Rose felt as if she was abandoning a puppy by the side of the road.

"I promise, Thackeray." She gave him a quick kiss on the forehead and left.

Luckily, Rose made it back to the house before her parents, but when they returned, she was in no mood to see anyone and headed for her room. She didn't care about what her parents did with their friends. All she wanted was to go back to the mansion, but she still had much packing to do. She looked down at everything strewn across the bedroom floor. Her room back home never looked like this, and as she pulled out her suitcase, she tried her best to put everything away neatly.

When she grabbed Edmond's jacket, she held it close to her chest, and tears fell from her eyes. He had been so gentle with her the night before. Rose carefully folded his jacket and placed it inside her suitcase. She looked over at the bed to see Elizabeth's dress and grabbed that as well. It took more effort to fit the dress inside, but Rose succeeded in closing her overpacked suitcase.

Just as Rose thought everything was ready to go, she spotted Elizabeth's diary on the nightstand. There was still one more entry for her to read. Rose picked it up, her hands shaking, and opened to the last pages. The words were hard to read.

Dear Diary,

I know not the day or the year in which I am writing to you. Everything around me seems to be changing so quickly, everything but me; you see I have awoken from a strange dream. In fact, I have been having strange dreams for the last couple of months now. In my dreams there is this girl. She is so beautiful, and I am jealous of her rosy auburn hair, and her blue eyes look so wonderful and new and full of life, unlike mine. The only thing I do not envy about her are her strange clothes; I prefer to stick with my dresses.

These dreams about her don't make any sense. Sometimes I see glimpses of her in the forest, in my home, and sometimes in my bed! When

I call out or try to approach her, she runs away from me.

I always wake up before I can reach her, but what bothers me the most is that sometimes I see her walking with Edmond. He looks so happy with her. I wonder if he was ever that happy with me. I feel like I'm going crazy. If this girl ever comes to be, I want her to be the one to give Edmond my diary.

The final chapter to my immortal life is coming to an end; I can feel it in my bones.

The words stopped there, and the rest of Elizabeth's diary was empty. Rose set it on her lap and took a deep breath. It all made sense to Rose now why she kept seeing Elizabeth. The answer was so clear to her. Elizabeth's words had helped her make up her mind. Rose's answer was definite now.

Chapter Twelve

Rose's last week in England was a blur. She visited gift shops that she hadn't had a chance to see and bought a few things here and there to bring back as gifts. But nothing seemed to interest her. She touched her lips, remembering the feel and taste of Edmond. Thoughts of their first night together ran through her mind over and over. She wanted to be with him again like that at least one more time.

Tiffany came up from behind her daughter and asked, "Something on your mind?"

Rose was startled but quickly collected herself. "Not really," she lied.

"Are you packed to leave tomorrow?" Tiffany asked.

Rose nodded ruefully. "Yeah, I just wish we could stay longer."

Tiffany sighed happily and smiled. "There will be another time to come back."

"Are you sure?" Rose was scared to ask.

Tiffany put an arm around her daughter. "You love England that much?"

Rose's eyes grew moist, but she held back her tears. "I do." When she said that, she was saying she loved Edmond and Thackeray.

Thackeray lay on the floor of his bedroom crying. Rose told him she would be back, but that was four days ago. Maybe she decided that it would be too hard to come back one last time. Maybe not coming back at all was easier.

"Get up," Edmond ordered as he walked into Thackeray's room. "You've been crying for hours." He looked about the room. "This place is a mess. Get up before you get filthy."

"She's gone!" Thackeray said, sobbing. "Rose is never coming back!"

Edmond was hurting, too. "I want her back, too, but you don't see me crying about it." In truth Edmond did cry; he cried late at night after Thackeray had gone to bed.

Thackeray sat up and dried his tears in vain. "How come you never paint or draw anymore?" he suddenly asked.

Edmond was taken aback by his question, surprised that he would even ask that. "That's none of your business."

Thackeray stood up and turned to face Edmond, angry now. "Well, I'm making it mine."

Edmond folded his arms, irritated. "You never tell me anything anymore, so why should I?"

Thackeray scoffed. "You didn't mind telling Rose about Elizabeth."

"Don't you dare say her name," Edmond warned.

Thackeray was swift to fire back: "Which one, Rose or Elizabeth?"

"Both," Edmond barked, grabbing Thackeray by the shirt.

Thackeray tried to free himself from Edmond's grasp. "Have you made love to her yet?"

Edmond twisted Thackeray's shirt even more. "What do you know about love? You'll never be able to experience it like me."

Thackeray didn't show it, but that was one of the most hurtful things Edmond could have ever said to him. "And it's entirely your fault!"

"My fault?" Edmond said with a laugh. "What makes you think that?"

"The potion—you made me drink it, remember?"

"I never made you drink it," Edmond retorted, fuming. "You wanted to. And I fail to see how that makes it my fault."

Thackeray squirmed. "Everything else seems to be, why not this?"

Edmond picked Thackeray up off the floor and held him with both hands. "I should have left you to die in the streets!"

Thackeray wanted to take it all back—every bad thing he ever said to Edmond, but insults seemed to be the only thing he *could* say. "And I wish you had!"

Edmond shoved Thackeray as far as he could and watched him land on the bed and roll off the other side with a loud thud. It was quiet for a moment as Edmond held his breath. "Thackeray, are you all right?"

Thackeray lay still on the floor.

"Thackeray, say something."

Finally, Thackeray moved. He stood up slowly, rubbing his neck, and sighed.

"I'm sorry about everything I said," Edmond told him. "Will you forgive me? I don't know what came over me."

Without turning around, Thackeray answered him. "For a moment there I died. I broke my neck, and for a second the pain was gone, but now it's back." He sighed. "I understand, Edmond. I don't think either of us meant what we said. Does that mean I forgive you? I don't know."

An uncomfortable silence befell the room.

"Do you want to go hunting with me?" Edmond asked.

Thackeray shook his head. "No, I think I'll stay behind. Besides, if Rose comes back, someone should be here."

Edmond placed a hand on Thackeray's shoulder and squeezed gently. "I really am sorry, Thackeray." He left his friend alone after that, closing the door quietly behind him.

Rose returned to the house with her parents early that afternoon. The house had been straightened up, and more of their belongings were packed. As they pulled up in the driveway, Alan and Diana's car was there, and they were waiting for them.

"Did you think you could go without seeing us?" Diana asked.

Lucas locked the car and walked up to Alan. "We've been so busy packing that we haven't had a chance to call."

"That's why you didn't answer. You were all out and about," Diana said. She then turned to Rose. "How do you like England?"

Rose smiled. "I love it."

Tiffany walked to the front door and unlocked it. "Everyone come inside and talk. It's hot out here."

Rose wandered up to her room and left the four adults alone. She didn't feel like talking to anyone and had much to think about. Even though she had made up her mind, her other options danced around inside her head. She grabbed Elizabeth's diary and stared at it for a long while.

When a soft knock sounded at her door, Rose looked up and saw her mother poke her head inside.

"If you want, Alan and Diana invited us over to their place for one last meal."

Rose thought for a moment. "No, I'll stay here."

Tiffany raised a brow. "Are you sure? Diana is making steak burgers."

It was tempting, but Rose had more important things to do. "Yeah, I'm sure. Besides, there is food in the fridge still, and I can always eat at the airport tomorrow."

Tiffany was surprised at this but respected her daughter's choice. "Okay. I'll bring you home something then."

Before closing the door Rose called out to her mother. "Hey, Mom, when will you and dad be back?"

Tiffany paused for a second to think. "Maybe not till late. Don't wait up for us, if we end up getting back later than expected."

Rose nodded and watched her mother leave. That could be the last time I see my mom, she thought to herself.

Thackeray sat in the great room playing with his wooden toy soldiers when the door to the mansion opened. He ignored it at first, but then he heard the soft pitter-pat of footsteps and looked up.

"Rose!" he exclaimed and ran to give her a hug. "I'm so glad you're back!"

Rose held on to that hug for as long as she could. "I told you I'd be back."

Thackeray looked up at her wide-eyed. "Are you hungry? Thirsty? Maybe you want to play with me?"

Rose chuckled. "What do you want to play?"

Thackeray pointed at his toy soldiers. "We can play war, or we can go outside and do something. Whatever you prefer."

Rose walked over to his toy soldiers and sat down. "Playing war sounds fun."

Thackeray quickly set up the game and explained the rules, which were simple, and they started to play. They sat there on the cool stone floor for an hour making jokes. Rose saw the enthused look on Thackeray's face and could tell he hadn't had a playmate for many years.

There was no talk of leaving or staying, just lively chitchat about their day, or things they wanted to do or see if they could.

Rose looked over at Thackeray, her soft smile fading, and asked, "Did you know who I was when you first saw me?"

Thackeray set a toy soldier down. "What do you mean?"

Rose tried to explain herself better. "In Elizabeth's diary she wrote about me. That girl she saw in her dreams was me. Did you know who I was when you first saw me?"

Thackeray was quiet for a moment and then nodded slowly. "I had a very good idea."

Rose had a hard time reading the look on his face. "And what do you think about it?"

Thackeray leaned back on his hands and sighed. "I think everything happens for a reason. I was fortunate enough to learn about you coming way beforehand. I also think that also helped me persuade Edmond to let you come back to the mansion. I never said anything of the sort to him, but I managed to change his mind in a different way, and that's why we invited you over."

Rose was happy to know he had made the effort to see her again. "Thank you for that."

Thackeray made another move. "Better luck next time," he said as he took down Rose's last soldier.

Rose laughed. "I need more practice."

At that moment Edmond walked in with a trail of rabbits tied to a thin rope.

"Rose," he stopped short, "you came back."

Rose stood up and ran to give him a hug. "I had to."

Edmond dropped the rabbits and held Rose close. "I'm really happy to see you."

Rose let go of him and picked up her bag. "I need to talk to you."

Edmond looked to Thackeray. He knew what that look meant and started to pick up his toys. "I'll go outside," he said and left the two alone.

Rose grabbed Edmond's hand and pulled him toward her. "We need to talk in your room."

Edmond wasn't going to resist and followed her.

"What do you need to talk to me about?" he asked after closing the bedroom door.

Rose answered him with a passionate kiss and wrapped her arms around his neck. "I really wanted to do that," she said.

"You can do it again if you want."

Rose smiled and laughed to herself. "Before we go any further, I need to give you something." She pulled Elizabeth's diary out of her bag. "Do you have any idea what this is?"

Edmond shook his head. "Is it yours?"

Rose made him take it. "It's Elizabeth's diary."

"Wait, say that again?" Edmond wasn't sure he heard her correctly.

"Elizabeth entrusted her diary to Thackeray before she left, and Thackeray gave it to me, and now I am giving it to you."

Edmond gripped the diary more firmly. "She kept this from me?"

Rose felt bad for him. "I think she did it for your own good."

Edmond scoffed and shook his head. "All these years, and this was right under my nose." He tried to give it back to Rose, but she refused.

"I can't," she said. "Elizabeth wanted you to have it."

Edmond was confused now. "If she wanted me to have it, then why did she have Thackeray keep it from me for so long?"

This is what Rose wanted to hear. "That answer is in there. In fact, all the answers to your questions are in there."

"You read all of it, I'm assuming?" Edmond asked.

Rose nodded.

Edmond placed the diary on his dresser. "I can't read this right now."

Rose grabbed his hand and squeezed it gently. "It's okay, you don't have to. You have plenty of time to read it."

Edmond laughed solemnly and let out a heavy sigh. "And how much time do we have? Are you staying or no?"

Rose's heart felt as if it was going to jump out of her chest. She was more nervous than on her flight over the Atlantic. "Edmond, I love you and Thackeray so much," she began. "I love my parents very much too."

Edmond didn't want to hear any more, but he forced himself to listen.

Rose brought Edmond's hand up to her lips and kissed his fingers. "I can't stay."

Edmond looked away. He feared if he looked at her he would break down and cry. "How much time do we have?"

"A few hours," Rose answered.

Edmond pulled Rose into a tight embrace and held her like that for a long while. His body was shaking, and Rose did her best to comfort him.

"What can I do to keep you?" Edmond whispered.

Tears rolled down Rose's cheeks. "You have me now, Edmond."

"Say it again," Edmond begged.

Rose wrapped her arms around him even tighter. "You have me now."

"No, say my name again."

"Edmond," she said, smiling.

Edmond picked Rose up bridal style and carried her to his bed. He laid her down gently and took his time taking off his clothes and hers. He wanted to enjoy this moment for as long as he could. There was no room for rushing.

They rolled around in bed, giving each other sweet kisses and enjoying the freedom of their naked bodies. Edmond was as gentle as he had been the first time and made sure her desires were fulfilled before his.

When they finished, they lay in bed for a long time talking. A single candle was lit but that was enough.

"Promise me you'll read the diary," Rose said as she rested her head upon Edmond's chest, listening to his heartbeat.

"I promise," he said, kissing the top of her head.

Rose sat up suddenly and reached for her phone on the nightstand. "I need to go. It's getting late."

Edmond sat up, resigned, knowing this time would come. "I'll walk you back."

They walked to the great room and found Thackeray sitting on the sofa reading. He sat up quickly when he saw them and put the book down.

"Is it time?" Thackeray asked.

Rose nodded. "Edmond is walking me back. Want to come?"

Thackeray surprisingly declined her offer. "I would love to, but it would be just too sad for me. I'd like to remember you this way, as you are now, standing here in the mansion. I'd rather remember you standing here than walking back to the house."

Rose walked up to him and gave him one last hug. "That's fair enough. Goodbye, Thackeray."

"Goodbye, Rose." Thackeray said, a look of misery in his eyes, watched her leave. To him it felt as if he was losing Elizabeth all over again. But there was a chance that Rose would return.

The sun was about to set when Edmond and Rose stopped at the edge of the forest. A cool breeze had made the temperature more bearable.

"You can still change your mind." Edmond said, seeing that the lights were off in the house and no one was home yet.

"You know I can't," Rose told him.

Edmond smiled, feeling desperate. "I don't know what you did to make me love you so much."

"I could say the same about you," she said as she kissed him.

Edmond played with a strand of her hair. "I'll wait for you forever."

Rose fought back tears. "I know you will." She took his hand and pressed his palm against her cheek.

Edmond brought Rose in for one final embrace and kissed her passionately. He felt a part of him leave with her as he let his fingers slip through hers and watched her disappear into the house. Only then did he weep.

The following morning, as Rose and her parents loaded the car, Alan and Diana came to make sure they made it to the airport safely.

From time to time Rose looked back toward the forest to see if Edmond and Thackeray were there, but she saw no one. She sighed and got into the car, wondering if she would return. She had college to think about now, and that would take time and money, and Rose knew she would have to work hard if she ever wanted to come back.

As the car started up, Rose looked out the back window and spotted two hooded figures standing at the edge of the forest. They had come, after all. Rose could only stare back as she slowly disappeared from view.

Years later, Edmond sat in front of the fireplace in the great room and scanned Elizabeth's diary. He had read it numerous times, but each time it seemed different to him.

The windows rattled as the brisk winter winds picked up. The winter that year was fairly warm, and the river had not frozen over yet, so the howling winds were comforting to Edmond's ears.

Suddenly, there was a knock at the door, but Edmond ignored it. The knock came again, and again he ignored it.

"Are you going to get that?" Thackeray asked, sitting up from lying on the floor.

Edmond grumbled. "It's just the wind, Thackeray."

When the knock sounded again, louder this time, Thackeray stood up and made his way over. He tried to open the door himself, but a gust of the wind prevented him from doing so.

Soon Edmond stood up, placing Elizabeth's diary on the sofa, and walked over to Thackeray. "It's just the wind, I'm telling you." Edmond opened the door and was shocked to see someone standing there. "Can I help you?"

The person standing before him was an elderly woman. She was bundled up and the cold didn't seem to bother her as she smiled at Edmond. "You haven't changed at all," she said in a frail voice

"Excuse me?" Edmond replied, raising a brow.

The elderly woman snapped her fingers. "Oh shoot, where are my manners? It's me, Edmond, your Rose."

Edmond stood there dumbfounded; his mouth agape. "Rose..."

Thackeray was quick to act. "Come inside, Rose. We've been waiting for you." He led her in gently, careful not to hurt her. "I'm so happy to see you."

Edmond closed the door and locked it, still trying to process what was happening.

"Oh, my," said Rose, "look at this place." The mansion had fallen into disrepair during her absence.

"Are you here to stay?" Thackeray asked.

Rose smiled lovingly. "Yes, I'm here to stay."

"Hooray!" Thackeray exclaimed, jumping for joy.

Edmond finally spoke. "Is what you say true?" he asked cautiously.

Rose took a seat next to the fire to warm herself. "Yes, Edmond, you can stop worrying now."

Edmond felt the pain that had been inside of him wash away in an instant. Even though Rose was wrinkled with age, he loved her all the same.

"What did you do after you left?" Edmond asked as he took a seat beside her.

Rose waited to speak until Thackeray was on the floor and ready to listen. "I went to college and studied to become a music teacher."

Edmond smiled at this.

Rose continued. "It took me a long time, but I managed to save up enough money and come back," she paused. "I was twenty-eight at the time."

Thackeray cocked his head to the side. "Why didn't you come see us? And how old are you now?"

Rose felt bad for admitting this but felt she had to tell them the truth. "I wanted to come see you, believe me, but I knew that if I did, I would have stayed. And I'm eighty-three now."

"What kept you from us?" Edmond asked, feeling hurt.

"During that time, I was engaged to someone back home, my California. His name was Richard."

Edmond was suddenly very jealous of this Richard, but he soon realized that Rose spoke about him in the past tense. "What happened to him?" he asked.

Rose sighed. "He died ten years ago."

"I'm sorry, Rose," Thackeray said.

Rose smiled at him to let him know that she was all right. "Richard was very good to me."

"Did you ever tell him about us?" Edmond asked.

Rose shook her head. "No, that's part of the reason I didn't come back until now." She thought for a moment, trying to collect the pieces of her past. "I came back a few times after that, but I was never able to show my face here. Can you forgive me?"

Edmond patted her frail hand. "There is nothing to forgive."

"Did you have any children?" Thackeray asked, suddenly curious.

Rose nodded. "I did. Richard and I had two daughters together, Hannah and Elizabeth."

Edmond smiled on hearing the name Elizabeth.

"They are at the house now. They know about you two. I told them a few years after Richard passed away." Rose wasn't sure how they would take this news, so she waited patiently for one of them to say something.

"When can we meet them?" Edmond asked.

"You both can tomorrow, if you want to," she said, overjoyed at their reaction.

"I would love that," Edmond replied.

The following month was pure delight. Edmond and Thackeray met Rose's daughters and together they sang and danced in the music room. Rose played the piano while Thackeray sang and Edmond danced about the room with Hannah and Elizabeth. It was a time for jokes and games and telling stories—the old days had returned.

The mansion no longer sighed in despair. Instead, she wept happily as joy was brought back inside her loving arms, but she was growing weary. Her bones were brittle, and the windows to her eyes were breaking one by one and being boarded up. The end of her desolate days was coming to their final resting place. It was time to say farewell.

One crisp morning as Edmond woke, he found Rose still fast to sleep.

When she awoke, he smiled at her and said, "Good morning, Rose." It felt good for him to say those words.

"Good morning, Edmond."

Edmond's stomach growled. "Are you hungry?"

"No, but I can tell that you are," she replied with a chuckle.

"Will you join me for breakfast anyway?" he asked.

Rose shook her head. "I'm still sleepy. I think I'll lie here for a bit."

Edmond nodded to this. "As you like." He kissed her forehead and left the room.

Rose lay in bed thinking. The embers from the fire were still glowing, and the burning wood could be heard crackling.

Suddenly, Rose saw someone all too familiar standing in the corner of the room. She brought the covers up to her face, scared that if she breathed too loudly or blinked, the figure would vanish.

"Don't be scared." It was Elizabeth. "I've come to get you."

"Why?" It was all Rose could say.

Elizabeth touched Rose's hand. Her touch was soft and warm.

"Just close your eyes. Everything will be fine, you'll see." She sang a tune that Rose had heard when she first arrived to the house. Back then it soundly melancholy, but now it sounded blissful.

After a few moments Rose drifted off to sleep, never to awaken again.

For a moment the room was silent. The embers died away, and stillness filled the void.

Edmond returned with a small bowl of fruit and sat on the bed. "I decided to eat in bed." He waited a few seconds, and when Rose did not respond, he nudged her. "Rose?" Surely, she couldn't have fallen back to sleep that quickly. Edmond set the bowl down and gently shook her. Still she did not wake. He swallowed hard and grabbed her wrist, checking for a pulse. When he found none, dread filled his heart. He had gotten her back just to lose her again. Fate was a cruel friend.

"No," Edmond wailed. "No, no." He started to cry. "I wanted to keep you, my Rose, forever." He buried his face in his hands and sobbed.

Rose was buried in the graveyard that day. They placed her beside Benjamin and carved her a headstone out of wood.

"This is what our mom wanted," Elizabeth said.

"She knew she was dying, so we came here with her," Hannah explained.

"This was her last wish." Elizabeth was sorry for having kept this from them.

Thackeray wiped his runny nose. "We can't change what's happened. I feel honored for being given the chance to know Rose."

Everyone looked to Edmond, who had yet to say anything.

He took in a long, drawn-out breath and slowly let it out. "Rose made the right choice. I'm happy for her."

A week went by, and Edmond sat alone in his chair sipping on a glass of wine. The drawing of Rose from so many years ago hung on the wall next to the fireplace. Edmond had done his best to preserve her memory.

Suddenly, a knock came to his door. He didn't bother to answer. Thackeray poked his head inside and assumed that it was okay to enter.

"She's really gone, isn't she?" Thackeray asked, walking up to Edmond.

Edmond didn't respond.

"What will you do now?" Thackeray asked.

This time Edmond answered. "I've been thinking about that all day. I think I will leave the care of the mansion in Hannah and Elizabeth's hands."

Thackeray's eyes grew wide. "Really?" He paused. "Wait, what are you saying, Edmond?"

Edmond took another sip of his wine. "I think it's time I leave, too."

"Are you certain about this?" Thackeray wasn't sure if his old friend was thinking clearly.

Edmond nodded. "Of course, you don't have to come with me."

This surprised Thackeray. "Don't be stupid. Of course I will come with you."

Edmond finished the last of his wine. "Good. Tomorrow morning then. Any later, and I might change my mind."

The next morning Edmond and Thackeray awoke early, just as they had planned, and walked to the old dock with Hannah and Elizabeth. It was mostly rotted away now, but they did not need it to slip their boat into the river.

"It was a pleasure getting to know you," Hannah said. "I will miss you."

"We both will, a lot," Elizabeth added.

Hugs were exchanged.

Edmond handed Elizabeth a rolled-up piece of paper. "Inside I have given you full right to the mansion. It belongs to you two now."

Elizabeth held the paper close to her heart. "Thank you, Edmond."

Edmond helped Thackeray into the boat first and then got in. He pushed away from shore, and they started on their way.

"Are you scared?" Edmond asked Thackeray.

Thackeray grabbed Edmond's hand and squeezed it. "I'm okay." He sniffled, trying not to cry.

Edmond knew that Hannah and Elizabeth would be fine and that they would take care of the mansion. He had no regrets.

Edmond put his arm around Thackeray. "We're going to see Elizabeth and Rose. We're going home."

As they continued, their skin started to sag and wrinkle, their bodies aging within seconds. And just like that, they turned to dust, their clothes falling in a pile, and an empty boat floated downriver.

About the author

Bridget Kathleen was born and raised in Columbus Nebraska, March 18th 1992. She now resides in the Twin Cities of Minnesota. Bridget has always been fond of forests and spent most of her summer days as a child exploring. In her spare time she enjoys going on walks, playing video games, sewing and playing D&D. Some of her hobbies are: cosplaying, reading, drawing and photography. Most of all she loves traveling and seeing the world.

www.ingramcontent.com/pod-product-compliance
Lightning Source LLC
Chambersburg PA
CBHW071241130626
46556CB00003B/1105